Another Love Discourse

also by Edie Meidav

Kingdom of the Young

Lola, California

Crawl Space

The Far Field: A Novel of Ceylon

Strange Attractors: Lives Changed by Chance (editor)

Another Love Discourse
a lyric novel

Edie Meidav

Terra Nova Press
NEWARK CALLICOON MATSALU

2022

ISBN: 978-1-949597-2-02

Library of Congress Control Number: 2022931687

published by:

Terra Nova Press
NEWARK CALLICOON MATSALU

Publisher: David Rothenberg
Editor-in-Chief: Evan Eisenberg
Designer: Martin Pedanik
Artwork by: Cecile Bouchier
Proofreader: Tyran Grillo
Set in EB Garamond

printed by Tallinn Book Printers, Tallinn, Estonia

1 2 3 4 5 6 7 8 9 10

www.terranovapress.com

Distributed by the MIT Press, Cambridge, Massachusetts and London, England

To all who survived these last years.

May the memory of those who did not
be a blessing.

Contents

Mourning: a cruel country where *I am no longer afraid.*

What I find utterly terrifying is
mourning's *discontinuous* character.

—Roland Barthes

And David sware moreover, and said, Thy father certainly knoweth that I have found grace in thine eyes; and he saith, Let not Jonathan know this, lest he be grieved: but truly as the LORD liveth, and as thy soul liveth, there is but a step between me and death.

—1 Samuel 20:3

Invite in the mess

so you might crave the order

that is mother

that is love.

To be engulfed

You of course tell
your story from wherever
you find yourself and hope
someone might hear.

Imagine the laws of life:
a mother birthing a tiny creature
on an eastern coast,
critter no larger than the letter T
in time, a life-form seeking not
just survival but thriving.
Imagine a little bug bit me, lower left cranium,
survival center,
and, ignoring protocol
because of the year of our shutdown,
I impatiently pulled it off.

Or imagine a game of chutes
and ladders and the thick
resounding of an echo chamber.

Your mother has died.
You are now motherroot for three daughters.
You have *been party to* a divorce.
You have moved several times.
Then slide into—! unprecedented
global pandemic (which is not the story
I will try to tell). Let us call it,
however,
the *ripcord*
(first shock when all of us
tugged
a parachute, the survival

wish) and then
the *float*
(in which we now live,
forever, prior rules
of time, space,
and communion
suspended).
Now the ripcord:
lost, atwirl
in memory. The float
remains.

You have been alone in isolation
with your daughters for a year.
Let's say
you also wish to believe
in if not wholly invent some new
language of love (thrill/calm,
belong/discover).
One narcissus-friendly definition: you love

the version of yourself
held in the gaze of the beloved.

Or:
a sense of security over time.

Or:
you love who and what you become in the light of the beloved.

Or:
you have come together to savor and learn,
and in safety, you heal each other's wounds
and then continue to discover more.

In this case, closeted,
a jewess who rarely outs herself,
a parent far from daughters,
the first time unmasked in a group of strangers,
the fog on the island three days straight.

This mother: find her out on a remote tiny island on which a mythical five-pointed stag as if out of Miyazaki wanders the center, once seen by an allegedly crazy writer who left his own leatherbound journal behind and sought to stay here (in the rough damp cabin in which I find myself, hard-hulled insects drunk on dust swept to the corner).

That crazed writer: wanting to fly solo through the winter, last seen with five cans of beans neatly stacked and many bottles of whiskey, nude with hands outstretched toward huge bonfire, burning another shelter rafter by rafter before the lonely pier.

Roland Barthes, a friend to this text, might tell us: the five cans of beans near the crazed writer's fire would be the *punctum*, the detail that punctures the heart of the picture with vulnerability and risk.

You might say that despite the way this island swallows people, offering them the craze of art, despite those who have gone missing, we all start to feel great hope here, as if the mythical five-pointed stag wanders the island bearing good tidings. The beauty of the tiny landscapes around these rocks could make you think that wherever the stag wanders, its hooves heal in the mossfairy forest whatever has been broken.

You might find yourself a mother who, among others, just buried her own mother with what Wordsworth calls in stuttered grief rocks, stones, and trees all around. Imagine her death coming soon after you had seen severed whatever you believed your own motherhood should be. *The myth of the airtight family.* Somewhere in the night of a twenty-year-plus marriage, there had stolen upon you different knowledge, earth rumbling, geysers no longer able to hold back: the rupture of myth.

What bedraggled camel can imagine itself back into that wedding in Vegas, walking with then-future husband before the woman taking photos, the shamaness who this last year would end up, briefly, your own mother's executor, but then, genial in glad rags, photographed you as a *couple* (myth and icon as Roland might say), *signifying* future love, connection, ease.

Your white dress, its rip, would that be the punctum? The dress bought cheap at a quinceañera shop in the Mission district of San Francisco, city named after someone who loved animals just as much as the one who became newish love in this last tiny, vast era.

That dress? It ballooned about in the wind. As if you were to stay forever (emotionally) (structurally) fifteen, child bride to a man seventeen years older. Clad disingenuously in white when so many incursions have been made, *the sign stripped of its signified*, dress whipping westward.

Ravishment

What does anyone want? Reader, here's the paradox: partly mothered, you made a vow to be there for three (3!) daughters once you had them.

Stayed in your new family long after the welcome mat became coir and then wire so they would have an intact family and you became no longer anyone you knew.

The lover must (wish to) recognize herself.

You instead became: a schreier, a crier.

Then made the break, as if hallucinating a different life.

New love arrived, and as one daughter points out, you became vital as a panther, happy and alive until the scourge hit.

And then your beau came to whatever we wish to call it—to be with you inside quarantine, foxhole, swannery. Your body then became a bridge over which the discomfort of others traveled, as, occasionally, a daughter balked.

I was bad to you, one says, *now I don't have a mother to myself, now I must share.*

The very means for finding new family (love sanctuary) was being undone by new family.

Try healing your own unmothered self by being a good mother. Yet approval must (always) be found inside. Try too hard, healing is undone.

The beds also: undone.

Bills: unpaid.

The book which this is not: unwrit.

A new night-hued puppy arrived: unwalked, wishing for the run in the morning instead of your writing this screed.

In the still of morning, a hawk often startles as you open the door, about to take the dog to the great joy of the brook where her nose sniffs others' noses and heels for rumors of travel, entire novels.

Say you wish for connection, your marriage dying for years for want of it.

Here tilts the paradox: good idea to up-end the apple cart? *Choose your marriage every day,* the wise friend used to say, advice you steadfastly ignored. Instead you repeated to yourself and your fried nerve endings *I don't believe in divorce.*

Riddle for the alert reader: can you love any part of your self if you make yourself a questionable parent by encouraging the end of a loveshorn marriage?

Skies both endless and heavy, you made the decision, as if discontinuity could bring children even more of the mother yours was not.

Zeno's paradox: the arrow flies close to its target but never quite meets its mark, the distance between tip and goal endlessly subdivided.

Obstacle to the love you covet might very well be the fact of the newish lover: one daughter finds his presence a great support, another blows soup bubbles at the question, a third riddles you (and the spike-head virus brings such queries home all too soon).

What is home for any of us? You get the thing you want, but too soon, at the wrong moment: is this not the structure of most comedy (or tragedy)? The devil forever in charge of timing. Time becomes this problem each of us must resolve.

As Roland whispers from behind the curtains:

Syntagmatic freedom is clearly related to certain aleatory factors: there are probabilities of saturation of certain syntactic forms by certain contents. This phenomenon is called catalysis; it is possible to imagine a purely formal lexicon which would provide, instead of the meaning of each word, the set of other words which could catalyze it according to possibilities which are of course variable—the smallest degree of probability would correspond to a 'poetic' zone of speech.

Q: What is rupture, genus personal?

A: To cut to the calendar chase:

February divorce, April cabin, June home purchase, August move from a temporary high-ceilinged apartment, February death of mother and last grandparent, collective isolation for a year in a new home meant to be a safe house for daughters and me, my employment site, the Institute of Roland Studies, about to shut doors, the prospect of hocking everything for a book on Roland ludicrous, teaching his wonderful love book to a community of pixelated faces who find succor, April's poisoned plants and swarming bugs, bulletholes in the writing shed, and leaving the daughters briefly with ex (X), as our collective isolation stretches, leaving for the first time for a scholar/artist retreat on a May island.

The calendar may jumble but facts stay stalwart.

Moves, home purchase, tenants to support the former, keeping the homefront stable for three gangly daughters light on their feet.

Order

Roland loved shuffling index cards. Roland (as he has come to be known in our house in which my work on him was meant to keep some roof over our heads, since it is true I have hocked everything, including the kids' own well-being and safety, to write a book on him which has not yet been written) kept playing with order. Any of his books could have achieved anything; how do you know when it should end?

That a story resolves somewhere: why not in another place?

Roland, who forever questioned the binary, would wish to undo the myth of classical narrative as understood in the contemporary writing workshop, to wit:

Someone has a goal and meets an obstacle.
Less interesting choices are made between a clear good and a stark evil.
The greater choice she makes—between a good and a lesser good or an evil and a lesser evil—reveals her character.
Greater pressure begins as a result of her choice.

We keep skidding ahead to the dénouement in which we (if not she) are all the wiser.

Events, setbacks, annoyances

Consider (a bit longer) the whimsy of timing. Wedding one blustery day in Vegas exactly a month before planes of unnamable uncertainty tore through buildings (on what Whitman among others called so lovingly Manhattoes, the isle on which he imagined deer prancing, before capital came to mark deep grooves through streets of numbered minds). *I'm from Vegas,* your X would shout, as if hefting his angry father's leather-strapped, smoke-tinged pawnbroker croupier box, his people hunted by pogrom yet miraculously of both Shanghai and Australia, generations of crapshooters and rebellious prisoners from deep within a shared wager (call it history).

In the worst arguments, he shouted: *you got to understand how crap plays, this is how we talk, this is how life works!* You met him in your slush-cornered college town as you pursued your undegree. Seventeen years older than you, he hung out in a petite diner downtown, having dropped out, liking the perversity of being an anthro grad student gone blue-collar, watching each year bloom new undergrads, living in a spacious empty room over a quick-order stir-fry dive. Having inherited a slim fortune, a scion cut out of the massive part of the family will due to his mother's intransigence.

I'm red-diapered blue trash, he said, wittily, deprived of the ancestors' huge legacy and so all the more scrupulous in clinging to ideals, a person having made an art of befriending new students and older more permanent scholars on campus while hoping to complete the never-finished dissertation, an oral history of truck drivers on two major northeastern corridors, 90 and 87, instead ending up one himself, a substitute truck driver, liking the urgency, camaraderie, fun stops, and long solo hauls of a dashed-line highway. Destinations often justify all means: the great unjoke of all classes, high, low, middling, the anxious, the uneasily wed.

I've watched you, he said, early in that diner, *even when you walk and talk with other people, you're always alone.* And in this comment, I felt so seen already that what we call—as Roland's beloved *Sarrasine* narrator says *my heart for want of better term*—my heart for want of better term bounded out of my belly where it usually descended and skipped somewhere down the road as if alongside another.

In the loving calm of your arms

Besides intercourse (when the Image-repertoire goes to the devil), Roland writes, *there is that other embrace, which is a motionless cradling; we are enchanted, bewitched . . . In this companionable incest, everything is suspended: time, law, prohibition: nothing is exhausted, nothing is wanted: all desires are abolished, for they seem definitively fulfilled.*

Roland solo in the country with his mother had the following habits:

7 AM: wake.
Make tea, feed birds in garden with crumbs, dust desk,
empty ashtrays.

7:30: listen to radio news.

8: breakfast with mother: two boiled eggs, toast, black coffee,
no sugar.
Buy local paper, then work 'til

10:30: black coffee and first cigar,
work 'til 1 PM lunch.
Hour nap, putter in garden, burn papers in garden or prepare a
box of index cards.

Work again from 4 to 7,
including a short tea-break.
Then water garden, play piano, have dinner.

After dinner, TV or writing notes on index cards and music.

10 PM: turn in and read until sleep.

Of routines such as these, he says they indicate class, and fails to mention the connection to mother he maintained for a half-century. Many of us indicate our maturity by the extent to which we stray from legacy; some indicate it by how well we stay in the embrace of mother values, father tongue, communal mischief. Note the possibility of 10:30: the burning of papers in the garden.

Alone

A volunteer French teacher in Morocco might play-act being aristocrat of the body yet Roland, guilt-prone, took pains so mother would never find out, the gap between scholarly mien and erotic proclivity only one direct reference ever: sunglasses hiding his black eye, souvenir of Biarritz where he was beaten and robbed on the beach.

Elsewhere, not published before Maman's death: *The art of living in Marrakesh: a conversation between a moving horse-drawn carriage and a bicycle; the cigarette is handed over and a rendezvous arranged, the bicycle veers sharply and speeds off.*

I too have known this rough trade and shrugged it off because it speaks more of flinging myself on the arms of the world, trying to find in any home outside what I could not inside. I replicated this trait with the daughters: forever taking them outdoors. Outside we went to find the mother found in playgrounds, forest, marine waters. The *oceanic.* The goddess held in the concord of friends playing games. Knowing what one does inside with a self yet knowing less what one does inside with others. Having mothered self from the outside in, I sought to give them the same.

But Roland? Well-mothered, he stayed indoors (with notable exception) enjoying his eggs.

How can a man follow need yet half-keep it from mother a whole half-century? He forsook most forms of activism, given his wish to reject the time's hysteria, as he called it, happy nonetheless to be called Marxist, but also did not pretend to be what he was not. Midlife, for instance, he told one friend he preferred camel drivers to camels.

Therefore he became a being with one foot at the closet door who loved saying every text speaks to us in five codes, and how we might listen to any text *as an iridescent exchange carried on by multiple voices on different wavelengths.* What he did for himself: he changed the very architecture, making of the closet, that impervious jail, something like a Gaudí fever-dream: melting, layered, graspable.

All along omitting the most intimate closet: Maman had to be spared knowledge regarding how he found love in any world outside her door.

Does sexuality undergird what he wrote? Some would say his lifelong illness mattered just as much if not more, a self forever in sanatoria, a being forced to report to authorities from the gurgling interior about the aspirational joys of normalcy, the injustice of forever standing apart. That slithery sense of never belonging. To talk to the healthy is to abandon part of oneself: the secret throbs.

Who among us can say we threw away a part of a surgically removed rib? Roland: tragic, flippant, happy after surgery, flung his actual rib-bone away. Ungendering Eve's binary, undone. Minorities, madness, prison, the marginal: his peers (like Foucault) write of and through prisms not unrelated to the queer (a double-negative circumlocution the more grandly closeted Henry James also favored). Sole direct appearance of Roland's queerness? Within his book on himself you find this:

The goddess H:
The pleasure potential of a perversion
(in this case that of the two H's: homosexuality and hashish)
is always underestimated . . .
It produces a more*: I am more sensitive, more perceptive,*
more loquacious, more amused, etc . . .

Henceforth it is a goddess, a figure that can be invoked, a means of intercession.

Every class of secret lives within every class, yet all bear a family resemblance: secluded, mystic, occult. And so what if Victorians used collective hush as a way to stir up the tribalism of families, binding them together, and our more psychologically fluent moment, so aware of the redounding of trauma, instead makes the revealed truth tear families apart? No matter. A secret pulses light through goddess figures as well as demiurges, shines within any flimsy structure we are here together trying to build, illuminating soft parts, silhouetting bones.

Identification

A memory from childhood: a bully squashing me, a body that felt giantesque. An unblood uncle, an unrelated friend of mother's. He had his own ways, but such is memory that at times even mother's hug melded with his, a fear she might crush me with goddess-size loneliness, need as if an enormity of avoirdupois, though she herself was only five feet two, the height of one of my daughters now.

Imagine that mother: she loved the painting by Reubens, the woman with a rose in her hair. Imagine this beautiful body, its face painted, washed, repainted so many times—*so you will think I'm pretty,* I heard her once say, plaintive to my father before they headed out—*I need to put my face on.* The face is what will be loved, bringing plaudits and bouquets to the transom. The face can be shown outside the domestic closet in which no mask is needed. The face is what the public understands, joining in some kind of communal orgasm of meaning: to sanctify if not meet that deepest need which we all have. To be loved for who one truly is stays closeted. How does anyone find a way to belong more to the grand tragic comedy of humanity?

Once I sat with father and mother on a boat not irrelevantly named the Queen Mary, docked in Long Beach. My mother appeared to be flirting with the accented waiter in front of my father and I made the fury vow easily made by adolescents: never be *that.* A rare solo travel with her: alone, she and I went to Muscle Beach in Venice, California, near its aspirational garlanded canals to watch vaselined bare-chested men inside their own chosen cage heave weights. *Amazing,* she said, *the titration and proportion of contemporary investment in*—and faded out, her protoscientific speech unable to mask libido. The men who like her (like me, like so many of us) had the habit of present pain toward the future gain of revealed grace. Roland would call it the signifying gym-body, or in the States we might term it the Calvinist capital of time invested.

Once she started to run out of time, at the end, the kindest caretakers understood her need to be appreciated. And so with love they daubed her with zany lipstick. (The clown magnifies what the audience fails to admit: the need to be loved. And I too have long felt myself in drag. The clown must please herself first, otherwise she stumbles. Do you *have* to wear eyeliner, my daughters always ask, as if I paint lines away from them and toward the outside world where I too could be taken offshore, lines moving off from our morning mussed loving hug, using a style ripped from the harsh econolines of the slapstick decade in which I came of age, clockhands seized in paroxysm around eyes meant all the more to take in the outside world.)

Mother's hair spiraled into dreadlocks and her caregivers lovingly fashioned it into, atop her head, two giant unquivering horns (past signification of jewess). Since all dying distills essence, my mother became love itself. Not just a person who appreciated solely the hope of love in some Zeno's paradox of an endlessly deferred future but actual love.

Imagine yourself mother's daughter in her last era, and you might find yourself with devoted caregiver bearing gentle steak knives, sawing to free hair from a head containing an active mind gone to watery islands. Her grown child, you wish to do your best as ever. Hold such a steak knife and of such moments the laughter of the gallows is born.

We might as well hang ourselves, laughing, giddy on asphyxiation.

Though your back quickly can become carapace, a great defense: your front is that slow pink fog of dissociation rolling in.

She went frail at the end, becoming her glowing eyes: she has not been buried long.

A few early truths: systems crush.
The need of others, whether tyrant or mothers, can squash.
And safety is to be found away, in the unblue light of outside, exile.

More first lessons: inside the tiny bulb of my baby uterus, the eggs of future daughters already lived inside mother's body as I was born, all sharing the same birth-month and now death-year, pioneering forward without that origin, their grandmother-body home.

Adulthood: become your own home of love, your being filled with fireflies of possibility.

Demons

Here on a northern island with St. Francislike new love,
who gently cups his hands around
moths, perfecting techniques for setting
them free (less and less recall
of Vegas mate clapping before my face,
to kill in a great coup one or three,
my startle justified by his
need, a rage at intruders who despoiled his Vegas
childhood, his father that canny blackjack dealer, all the fire I can
understand, yet still the PTSD sings)
arrived here, May as the ripcord
loosened, on a canting boat.

We left for this period our
H O M E—
ruptured marriage,
dead grandmother,
ecotenant and other animals,
and the need to keep
abode straight
for three daughters
and arrive
on a new island of reckoning,
honeymoon/survival
energy shading into sparking
joy and the dream of
stability.

The past year lifts,
in which we all roomed together
in a rambly parsonage
run poorly by me
as a boardinghouse

with unusual tenants,
the only place (too big
to afford) which I could find near
schools no daughter ended up
attending, with new love
and lost mother,
all rupture, death, and life housed
together this year
of the great float. A small bug worked
its way over all of us:
call it unrest.
No paradise anywhere:
the isle's
mossfairy forest sighs,
needing none of us.
And yet a crown of thorns tightens;
I cannot stop feeling
every word fights death,
my brain has no time.

Flayed

Apparently deer and possum swim to this island, as can chipmunks. All might ramble here when tides are low. Imagine an ocean filled with swimming deer trying to get to this island and its covert vantage. There is a trail I misheard as *the booby trail*, as in: you are a booby if you get lost, because get lost you will. This path I love taking is marked just enough that I keep my faith. It is *the buoy trail*: faded mercurochrome pellets tied to trees amid scrubgrass and ocean breeze. I keep trying to ring the island but give up halfway: my motivation puts on its usual show. No completion. Some thornring of fire seems to be circling my head.

Look how you hurt the kids, my Vegas mate kept saying, self-willing blindness to his part in the passion play and our transfiguration, *you broke up their home.*

Soon and then later, eventually, all three daughters said they were glad for the divorce, as they felt health return. Let life expand to fill your dreams, said the divorce doula, a friend who made herself available in ways that still tentpost my heart with their generosity.

This last spring, at middle daughter's coming-of-age ceremony, held in a basement with sputtering light and rain hitting gutters hard, an old friend said to Vegas mate: *Your relationship is not failed! That's one idea, that a relationship fails just because it ends. But there are failed marriages which are relationships that stay unloving and intact for years: it is more a failure that they don't stop—*

But Vegas mate interrupted, legs wide, a wrestler's stance: *Not where I'm from!* His birthplace Vegas is famous for quick relationships and yet his lineage is Australian prisoners who rebelled, caring for fairness. *A relationship ends, it is a failure!*

May I say I prized this loyalty in him and value it still? Our daughters knew that, irascible as he could become, he would never leave. The foxtail sticks. Roland says *the wrestler who suffers in a hold which is reputedly cruel (an arm lock, a twisted leg) offers an excessive portrayal of Suffering; like a primitive Pietà, he exhibits for all to see his face, exaggeratedly contorted by an intolerable affliction.*

Before we wed, all those years ago outside a plasticine set of Vegas columns, X asked me can an eagle get married to a rock?

In the land around this question, girded by flamethrowers, loyalty trumps autonomy. Never could I identify with the shark or eagle, animals to which he compared me as if lovingly. Hadn't I always loved more the dolphin, panther, butterfly? Safety: the greatest shapeshifter. Yet the hope for refuge (impregnability from all you have not invited) might make a person speak. While the wind will not be ignored, shaking overladen branches threatening to fall on a ramshackle roof.

The you that is I that is we: the hope of all writing, that we might learn to do this dance together.

In dreams begin responsibilities

Realizing that to identify with your father at age eight made sense. You wanted to process things the way he did, to be him, to not be that icon: *the shouting, enraged woman*. (His fingers, stiffening, cool blue, on the driving wheel. Father who had just left mother holding towel to chest, black ringlets pouring down, as if in a last Italian aria from *Sarrasine*, while he tripped lightly down the stairs, as if he played clerk in the end of that keen and now less-cited but crucial Delmore Schwartz story. Your mother shouting from the veranda at him. He, already gone.)

(The lack of emotional commensurability. The one-sided communication. His lack of attending an inner wound made outer, all that she needed to say.) In other ways, you wished to resemble him. How he gave succor. His broad head and pacific blue eyes of equanimity. To be sure you had a roll of quarters in your pocket when you went out in the evening, ready to hand to the errant or lost. Unafraid when finding a homeless man sleeping in the back of your car. Never kicking anyone out. Instead offering tenancy, at least a ride.

Imagine being that father. To sit on a bench in East Africa (hoping to create renewable energy for others) and to open your arms wide and smile disarmingly as three bare-chested men approach, each bearing on their shoulders long spears. They return the smile; you get to survive. Socialist, working any job, be that father connected east and west to the world, who met beggars, waiters, bankers, parking attendants, businessmen as equals. Drive through Beverly Hills in the rain, laughing, garbage bags strapped to the roof of your station wagon. Become that unusual beast back then: an energy pioneer, awarded and saluted by the capital of capitol. Age does not always tarnish idealism. Be that provider, open your home to the wayward and lost. Averse to confrontation, merry and jocund, have a wayward eye yet be a person frequently swindled.

Imagine yourself that father's daughter. Undo the work of Vegas mate who sought to make of your father an evil effigy in young ones' minds.

Your words a plea. *Please know your grandfather was admirable,* you tell them, *generous, kind.* You wish his memory to be a blessing. *If I have done any good for you, much has to do with my ma, whom you remember, yes, but also with my gentle father, the one you mainly recall dying.* Is it best to die long before a mate, which was your father's wish? Yet during his dying he cried out to you: *I am nothing but a burden to your mother.* Uncle Rick once told me the same: *dependency enrages your mother.* How can you be different?

One daughter you teach to drive in a nighttime parking lot, alone until a deer comes to watch, heraldic copper but ghostly amber at the periphery, evanescing. Does it matter that grandfather's name translates as *deer*? The night animal nods approvingly before bounding off under sodium lights. *You are a good driving teacher,* daughter says, *so chill.* You mention that grandfather taught you patiently how to drive, hoping honor might cling to the ghostly brow of the salt-miner's grandson, saying you channel grandfather's calm. The magnet braid of legacy: what ends up clinging?

Late in life, you sense the weight of all your mother had to handle. His depressive moments, his wandering. *When I am with you,* your father used to say, *you know it is the best moment in my life?* (Such burden on one psyche alone could train a person to run.) How old were you? Eight? *What is my purpose in living? I have fulfilled my biological function, just as a salmon does, and now can swim upstream—*

No, Daddy, no! you might say, cartoonish and peddling furious toward cheer *there are so many reasons to live!* Invent cheer, invent invent, eight years old: there are so many reasons to live. *Don't die!* A lifetime of wonder (or its opposite, a sense of doom) already opening in the young coach.

Fade-out

Don't forget: this may always be the favorite command of early spring when you easily mistake the burls of dying trees for squirrels, who do their clownish best, standing stockstill. Everything this second tends toward becoming gentle tendrils of green or some dark furtive knotted nest.

Everything collapses.

It is here, the formal beginning of the big, long bereavement, Roland says in his diary: notecards he began to keep mourning the loss of his mother.

Do the dead care what words we pitch in with the stones? Under duress, I tried penning a eulogy in my mother's house. Only three moons later, the home would be quickly dismembered, as if the funeral cakes were not to furnish a too-quick wedding, as in Hamlet, but rather Uncle Rick's future infinity pool. Tears with quick salt would soon be invested in the natural seawater swim my Uncle Rick would build using the home's cremains.

California forever dreams Shangri-La: *natural luxury yet magically using no resources.* Or, as Stevens asks *is there no change of deąth in Paradise?* Of grandmother's home, soon to be dismembered, youngest daughter, sentimental, would have reason to say: *my one permanent place, does it have to go?*

Under duress, at my late father's desk, the house still sturdy, I tried penning a eulogy. Who knew we would all soon be penning eulogies? Ripcord and float would come. Our collective lives would come to resemble what my mother's heirs began to do: over videocalls, heirlooms sorted, belongings become trashed black bags thrown in cacophony down the stairs, distressing the earth and a last surviving tenant in mother's basement. Some homes, like some writing, stay bare to create the future, while others hoard tokens of the past.

At my father's desk, under duress, in his study filled with foreign coins, obsolete how-to scientific tech manuals, its windows beat by plums for which my friend and I had risked death—climbing out on Spanish tiles, defying Aesop to reach branches, eros over thanatos, our song of youth—under duress, I tried penning a eulogy to my mother, having just seen her unspirited body, lipsticked, dark-ringleted, no longer Reubenesque but dead, stripped of her sparkle—in that study, under duress, I tried penning the eulogy (which due to a miscommunication Roland might have enjoyed, entered neither funeral speech, an act in which he half-believed, nor the funeral brochure, a mythological relic we late pharaohs create as if an ample enough hoarding to hold all memory).

I tried writing a survivalist's oxymoron, the nonfatalist eulogy, my hand trembling at words implying hope.

Yet nothing made it in: not those words, not these, nothing, no, every proscenium gapes. However I might celebrate her remains a giant gaping maw: the words that might have been. Uncle Rick and my brother and everyone forgave me, but O dear reader! A born mute, unwanted, unmothered until late, I ended up as ever a stammerer at mother's grave.

Absence

The last sense to go is hearing, apparently, but was mother present, any way we understand it, there at a funeral under California skies oddly unblue? My father had been buried a decade before at the same site and the sky went cerulean as his eyes, vast and forgiving. Yet when mother was buried, skies misted over mercury earth, vapor dense and violet as if touched by her gaze until the cloudburst at final eulogy: it seems too easy—a cliché (cast-plate click from the print factory of images)—until anyone recalls her magic.

Some people's dazzle comes from singular piquancy and others' from the combo platter. My mother: eternal student, biologist, inveterate teacher, party-thrower, community-gatherer, protoprofessional artist, drama and film impresario, dance teacher, frailer and yet more beautiful each year, skin silken, eyes essential. Having risen as a child under the poky umbrella of an era in which an immigrant family's vexed aspiration justified cruelty. Her mother: critical, daunted by dint of generation, cleverness throttled toward gossip and manipulation. Father: descended from Odessa shipbuilders with the broad ribs of boats, one of 350-odd people born on Ellis Island, having left school in the third grade to work, a master of benign diligence, almost illiterate. Each year, a birthday card arrived my way: xoxo and his name, Fred *and that's all he knows how to write,* the cruel echo sung by thwarted grandmother, her sharp blue eyes and pink asp of a tongue on constant campaign to denounce husbands or kinfolk, even daughters, never son or nation.

Both parents of mine: the ones who got away, jumping from vast herds. Every zebra is bred for loping off from threat but some young edge their tribe, ready to escape. *Hello?* (And already I think of leaving. You too might wonder if you could love.)

Tell us about your first break-up,
someone asked here on the island last night,
on the tiny platform on which I write,

all guests crowded onto it to see
one of these famous island sunsets.
I've never been left, I said with conviction, *it's pathological:*
that fear of abandonment.

It is true.
In the marrow, seek out those who defy physics,
those with a gravity that seems to transcend mortality.

Perhaps you too have it: the *myth* of the person who will never
leave. When our molecules forever jump
from my hand to your eyes to your hand;
meaning transforms, slippage always, and yet:

too many childhood moments
with some new
beloved arbitrary
temporary caregiver
spirited away
(and I watching from the window,
my punctum the broken frame).

This spring, non-uncle Rick has been chewing over the phrasing of his friend's tardy memorial stone, making me his bystander as ever, infantilizing my lost mother. An ashfield tickles the throat, that funeral soon before the ripcord when I forswore touching the hand of new beau. Untouching at the funeral so love-meaning might stay ours alone, private. Untouching so that nothing, as in a fable, could scissor the grandmother-root for my gaggle of girls. Sun glimmered for a second before cloudburst. My mother's mercury earth rose up; words fled. Did she care? For lack of eloquence, I would have been fired, for bad expression alone. Hang god, hangdog, whatever—words? I had none.

Reader, can you understand?

Always I craved her body.
And then sometimes,
it was too much upon me
heavy suffocating me on a bed in needy hug.

I was born, I drank milk, I spat, I suffered.

My first story—I was lying but she typed it, a rare moment of attention. *Inside your belly, almost born, ready, I hung, in a brown paper lunch bag, and whenever you drank your coffee* the stuff that made you go round the sun faster, mother, so you could work harder and better earn the love of outside people, men and superiors in the world outside, your own metaphor for your own soon-dead, never-approving mother *I spat it up.* Upended, I spat up the tube all that instant coffee my mother drank, and inside her I lingered, banged about, a being upended, as if inside the brown-paper sack lunch our father made whenever he happened to be home, showing his love by how he scored a circumference around the globe of the entire orange's peel.

She went to work first among forensic anthropologists and lab biologists and then later tech billionaires:

for a while, the only one in her family to have gone to college

stomping to work among neurodivergent biolab technicians wrinkling their noses at her lemon musk, high heels, huge sprayed dark hair, sheath of heavy necklaces, a splendiferous multicolor drag of sorts, a woman who in their boys' club clattered right in. Thirsty for love yet solipsistic, the narcissistic wound left in her by her mother a gift lending her the glam armor of confidence. A woman impressive not just to me. In this way, reader, mother's workaholism became my dearest teddy, a lemon musk you could scent for hours if you knew how to linger just the right way in the after-corridor.

Performance

More about absence, which is really death, which is really theater: I once worked for a performer boss (wait for her life sentence) who first said *we must make the act of theater special because you are asking people to sit in a small oxygen-less place for a fixed set of moments*: a definition of life or anti-life. So theater must be superabundant, vital, overflowing.

How moving that my mother's unlined unaged lemon-water-sipping theater son (present hocked for future and past), who works as a seller of mildewing books and does sit-ups behind the cash register, who finds life in being called for roles, who quotes himself saying, early in their deep friendship, to my mother *sorry you like father figures more, can I at least be your child figure?*—by her last bedside, a final gift of art, her art-son performed the play she had written for the dramatic writers' group she taught, the oxygen tube's gurgling pump the swish of mortal seas.

Roland would have understood this group and her loving gaze. Art, at the origin of the word, comes from Sanskrit, Greek, Latin, a mash-up of *manner, mode, skill, preparation, weapon, business.* Surveying her group, a soldier fending off death, my mother knew all art's rich meanings and how they suffused her blood.

Studies have shown novelty and danger—as in walking a tightrope—heighten both our sense of beauty and our attraction to the next face we see: such fact alone might argue toward breaking (conventional) form. Consciousness loves contrast, as Uncle Rick intoned. Toward mother's end, Rick invited her out for art's full risk. On mother's lap, she carried a portable box of hissing oxygen, front row at the theater as she loved, face dramatically pleasured, and only for a second entered rigor mortis, legs sticking straight out, before returning to life: contrast loved consciousness a little too much.

Would you die to watch something artful, knowing pleasure and freedom?

The last play I saw near her had to do with three generations of women sussing out the American diaspora. Having dropped her off with oxygen apparatus and Rick, I stayed held back by ushers in the lobby, watching a tiny screen about misbehavior, the corridor's lemon musk letting me know our last shared moment of art. Mother, are you with me now?

Theater gave her
oxygen. Her funeral—the feeling
she watched us all from above with joy
at our best true performance: love.

Fulfillment

Ripcord brings about the great
float and a blizzard falls

on the land. People
rediscover touch and

slowness, there is dread
and gold, raised flowerbeds

are ordered. At night in the
messy parsonage, they sit

on a burst couch furred
with the blessing of animals,

making up songs as if
to send out on the airwaves.

As if to sing is to be seen
by possibility itself.

Pigeonholed

Weekend before the great tugging of our collective ripcord, a person I admired but only partly knew lay down in her allotted five minutes in the women's gathering and bravely removed a hospital-color bra to show hospital-created breasts, said there was nonetheless one brave little neuron that had made its way, asked us to touch her breasts here, saying *symmetry is very important to me, touch me on one side then switch,* the ten women gathered for the weekend, her longtime friend asking, *if I press here, can you feel it.* I had never felt younger or more immature than burrowing in next to my large friend, feeling the animalcave warmth of her, unable to touch. Feeling not prohibition yet reserve. People who had asked to see me naked or had touched me in ways I had not wanted. Whose bodies had a certain flop and overextension not dissimilar to that of Uncle Rick who had invaded my own. You can stay in place and still flee. How does one rework that neural pathway?

Just touch my periphery, I had said, when it was my turn, *sing, anything, songs of praise.*

You are held by a river, you are safe, one started singing a song that means a lot to me, or at least it sounded like it, *b'shem hashem, in the name of the name, this angel is near you, Rafael, Michael, Uriel, Shekhina.* And the neat woman who had been in the next bunkbed had played a video of an earnest bearded man singing *I am blessed by the help of a thousand angels, softening my way to you* and this she sang now. She overachieves and pushes; I understand, we practically copulate in our love of work. Workaholism is a wonderfully never-ending highway. When it was my turn to dance, I didn't know how to soften my head: a feeling it would all collapse.

Adorable

No one ever wishes that anything (believed) good ends, including health, including love. Roland unfastens storytelling to say every sequence is made up of small nuclei *which always involve moments of risk* and that *precisely, at every one of these points, an alternative—and hence a freedom of meaning—is possible.* Each moment: attend it!

Early in the relation with new love C, then living far away, out west, I kept looking at the marks on my hands and body and thinking: how can I be loved? *Wouldn't it be silly,* he said, *if you were all that you are, and I let a few lines keep me from that? When you have been my dream since I was so young?*

The thing we fear with age difference is that we exist on different timelines, that one of us will skid into a different metaphysical vista than the other, that the core wound—of being fundamentally unlovable, of being bad—will be revealed.

In marriage, you pray to the gods of connubial bliss with both good works and faith. Calvinism would say the lack of grace becomes evident. Judaism would say that everything depends less on faith than works, that you can perform sans faith: some rabbis lack all belief.

Hence the scene of my prior marriage, the *Fiddler on the Roof* scene: *do I love you?* the wife sings at her philosophical mate before citing a litany of unseen domestic labor on his behalf, the bond of hard yokage. What happens when you forget how to replenish? Our old-world marriage had started to have this flavor, the crisis of faith right before the wife turns to us, her audience, and asks: *do I love him?*

Try to be a good person, best you can, act by sublunary impulses with a strong code of ethics, but forever your act binds you laterally to the community. Forgive the ghastly echo: work will not exactly free you but does bring you to the threshold.

As in a promiscuous bathhouse, jews cruise chances to overwork: the joy of working yourself to the hilt! Come to the edge of your stamina, hava nagila, go beyond!

Nine ways to escape psychic distress, said the mystical school in which I partook during my early twenties: panic, gossip, overwork, cruelty in a relationship, toxomania, gluttony, sensuality, crime, another I forget. *Even zen monks drink a drop of sake,* said my effervescent long-ago mystic-school mate, the one I didn't wed, a man twenty-seven years older than I, a living-health testament to the fruits of working hard on oneself, almost eighty but feeling himself aging in reverse, in a note last week joking that he'll be *near seventeen by the time we see each other!*

A repeated activity of long duration, not without risk: find yourself yet again sitting in the ostensible driver's seat outside your daughters' house, your former home shingled, stump-hued, wind-bleached. This house an overdetermined sign. You are awaiting transition: daughters leaving father's home, returning to yours for the week. Phone clock's digits tick toward numbers where they least belong; most waits of this nature can feel like hell's own infinity loop, a journey without terminus.

Finally, one daughter appears, bearing no bag of her own needs but rather a photo. Find your photographed self, younger than new love, beaming into your current self. Imagine: your face and torso caked not just with the unpassage of time but with actual Andalucían mud, you and two women striking mysterious poses—their names linger, one tall, one short, a moment carpet-bombed into your post-divorce waiting car from the time when you and X in uncertain honeymoon traveled to a Spanish art colony. Every couple seems to have at least one mode of near-excellence: the mode X and I employed best had to do with freedom. Untethered in travel, we did better: our lives when stationed resembled a three-legged race, tied by burlap together, trying to hop along, falling in order to inch toward any task.

Look! Imagine daughter pushing photo of past self your way. A person could feel undone by such an unexpected apparition of the past, thinking X wishes to disburden himself of memories of your past together. *You don't want this?* daughter asks. No, yes, sure (find yourself saying). *He has piles of pictures. I argued with him twice to get them, he didn't want to give me even one. He says the photographer owns the image! But I saw such a nice photo of you, you looked healthy, looking out a train window, smiling as if you didn't know you were being photographed, I really loved it, he wouldn't let me have it.* You might be mature for one moment. Let him have his life, his memories, his choices. *He says he keeps them to understand why he had us.*

And daughter #3 means kindness, she becomes a gravy train about your past before you were a mother or even wife, coming back and back again with still more handfuls of photos. *He said he'd make you a copy of the photo I wanted, he says O yes she was mad at me here and I was mad at her here.* Your maturity wanes. He is entitled to his memories, you might say, but need no more knowing. What the class after divorce court had advised: *don't let your child become messenger, spy, battleground, weapon.*

So what emerges from the prized-from-fist release of photos? In which struggle do you engage? Idealistic as it may yet sound: say you lose the battle for peace, can you still win the war for love? The reverse probably could be asked as well: lose the battle for love, but win for peace, or do all the terms blend? Are they the same, peace = love, a fundamental attachment our greatest leaders have known, and (our) (my) not having recognized their equivalence probably helped lead to the current mess.

Image

One request in childhood—only one.
Picture, age five, lying on mother's
scratchy plaid couch, in her holy
of holies, the office,

just to be near as she typed,
(saying): *can I go to an art class?*

Imagine the fancy: an art class!
What might that be? To see
yourself raising a hand
so you might talk
art with other artish people!

My daughter this last summer, excited at an outside dinner in desert compound (old abode of newish beau) in which a few creators live. A dinner enchanted, under fairy lights, hearing the darling neighborwoman rise into prophecy:

you'll see, one day, you'll be among artists
and you too will find you make
sense inside this tribe.

What a paradise! your childhood self thought, a place to make sense. *Art class!* (A berth in which a person could be some messy self. The understairs basement room where you stored the found starfish for which you cared when you were all of five, the starfish you ended up killing in its tissue-lined shoebox home with your ignorance and neglect in the place your mother called the arts and craps room.)

But on her couch, you imagined such heaven—uncrapulent lovely artish souls!

Did mother know that by asking for art
(mode, manner, skill) you asked for bliss?
She kept typing. The death ever-present in parenthood:
I too as a mother often
fail to listen or mishear the key:
I might alert the call-button of distress, or let
my mind associate what it should not.
Why does it cost so much
to listen deeply to another?

Mother's case: at home she typed, and unhomed on every vacation hefted an ancient briefcase, its skin once a cow's, filled with onionskin drafts, containing her brain as an expatriate before computers went portable. A dissertation representing undying

work, the chimera
granted a person: eternal
belonging
(meaning) (a link to another)
(mother)
(meaning).

A lab biologist, one of her early deigned-female jobs involved feeding research data. Strips of paper with binary punched code inserted into the hungry slot of a room-size wheezing Cray computer. Love biology, you love how even human-made things are created. Brilliant mother forever

asking a man
a piquant
question with debutante's tremolo.

Feeding herself into that system with its output that unicorn: the female scientist. Wishing to be recognized, that she might be known for the web of her mind threading connections, time's silver light playing her well.

That one request for an art class
rose like others unvoiced,
undulating in wind. Take your wraiths
of unmet
wish and make of them,
if you will, a ghost
forest with
moss clambering.

Roam
brinks to find fulfillment. You too may have had a dream
recurrent and involving:
picking self up under legs
to fly out over
villages ringed by flame,
those you can save if your hand stretches far
enough. Everyone
could catch on. Hands allied we'd fly, saved from
scratchy couches, the magical power
ours if only you keep recalling it.

(Until late I believed I could fly.)

Unlike her mother, mine was never heartless. Her good works legion: unlike her own, she did not make me clean my sick, nor painted my groin with iodine so stark, the red would tell kids I had touched myself.

Jealous, true, of absentee father's care for me: she and non-uncle Rick
shared belief
in love as scarcity economy, both
wanting the attention
of the man considered great,
my father. Yet she took
care of doctors, shots,
tabbed sheets marked MEDICAL HISTORY.
Ran the house,

and somewhere her affection lay
in wait 'til I tumbled into maturity

(which rests largely
in noting that people love
best they can with their own
art, mode, timbre, peacefulness).

Once, alone in the gray east, age four, dizzy and sick, home from school, I woke to find no one in the house, wandered as if out of body. Sad and confused (some term these ideal states in which to create first fiction) I dialed some number found on the counter, knowing it bad to interrupt mommy at work, inventing the reason: *sorry, I don't know how to open this soda*.

Reader, I must have been scared.

Knowing too it was wrong for me to be sick, for a body to fail—wait and see what destiny offers! To ask anything beyond my allotment. The arbitrary day caregiver she'd hired had stolen things, it turned out, a woman fled with mother's own typewriter. Later, that fact—mother's lost work—was the story that mattered.

From her, I learned not to speak.

And yet that magical moment playing with big red and blue floor letters at Montessori while other kids knew to be outside:

The beguiling code revealed! To get to read.

Enter memory with me if you please: as a child, I believed in a new personal invention that would make reading chairs unnecessary. What would such an invention help?

Imagine you were chairless. People would then care less (about you and/or reading) and so the act of taking in words would stay yours alone. A private act: rest forehead on school desk. Scent lemon wood soap, lay book in lap, bend one knee behind, foot poised, hook ankle behind the other, become an ostrich of reading, hide your face. In this way, no one would ever bother you.

Read until you were ready or numb enough to join the world. As in that recurrent dream, the other belief: if I could just take anyone's hand and fly with them, we could surmount their problems.

Later, all beliefs joined: chairless, I could read others' needs and then save everyone all the time.

Inside thrummed
the beat: under no circumstance displace
anyone. Don't even take up the space
of a chair. Hide and never be sought.

(Do you ever get a chair at the table?)

You too may have been one of
this village. You can learn to speak inside
by reading: this is writing as
Roland understood.

Mute until late, I only realized I
could speak to a group of
others late in the game,
seeing paragraphs unfurl as I spoke them—
in graduate school, others
laughing
at a joke I made
in a classroom. No longer
the lisper

non-uncle Rick told me I was,
no longer mute with avuncular Rick the lost
slithering over me, but someone who could summon
words that beforehand would flee,

little snakes out
from between my toes,
hollow chest, strawfilled belly,
anywhere you might find yourself later

gravid with inspiration,
divine energy,
knowing finally the purest love
from your parent at her funeral,

iron earth risen to meet you
not too late, as you touched
the shoulders
of your three daughters:

a tarnished motherroot can still shine, once revealed.

Fade-out

How sad—or rich and mature?—to see hopes attached to the start of all relationship change luster. All relations risk becoming husks of empty rites unless you stay aware enough to nurture the secret little green tendril of change inside the nub.

Sometimes when responding to others' work, I find myself returning to the one simple concept: all story furtively aspires to be detective fiction. The reader is the detective and yet, also, the buried treasure is the reader's increased understanding. We are always on the hunt for truth. In this way, the response to any written work becomes: what buried secret will emerge as one reads?

A Hansel-and-Gretel crumb trail resides in what has been left unsaid. Poets who travel into writing narrative find that no longer is all information simultaneous, frontal, as in an ancient painting in which action is understood immediately. The opposite also stays true: prose people lurching into poetry do well to omit the need to give all background. Instead, they learn the great generosity of the demo track in music or Picasso's minimalism at the end of his life. Avoid giving descriptors, allow the audience to fill in, to find their own inner tug at these words: *mother, friend, hand.*

Do we each have the right to hold certain memories sacred? Mark a certain land holy? That no one may there tread. In a land of Buddhist monks, border issues thrive: you remove sandals to enter a temple, monks offer sustenance which they have blessed—say, a pineapple half-moon—and you choose such transubstantiation (the food to which they have offered something divine) that it may cross the border of your body. Such borders are also mystically semantic, around the boundary of each word's meaning, each realm of knowledge.

Most of the time, we consume knowledge the way certain monks consume food. There is, after all, a monastic meditation on the disgusting nature of food: that we find rotting matter, whether carcass, seed, or vegetable, and with pistonlike nature chew it with blunted bits of calcium in our mouth before swallowing the formed pellets into a sack resembling something like a years-long unwashed cesspool. This body the vessel for ethereal forces, and yet we create immateriality solely through the material: the goal is to become aware of our greater alignment with whatever luminosity never changes form.

Attain samadhi by this method, some say. Transcend the body, note your hand paused midway between plate and mouth. See the endless emptiness of all effort and so find yourself liberated, free to choose the path of aligning with greater forces.

As you go through photos and paragraphs of past relationships, your material memory, as you cull them, what do you consign to the cesspit of amnesia? What do you keep central?

Give birth, approach a new friend, enter a new relation: in such moments you might find the buried joy of discovery. Extend your hand and your own being changes. So what happens when you choose to retract? To build a wall. To say a relationship ends. You don't have to have been divorced to know what it means to say no to someone from your past. Yet who then do you become? What new self do you declare behind freshly painted walls? How does your spirit not shrivel in a garden so quickly shaded?

Declaration

I have made the exact mistake Roland and therapists warn against: confusing the structural for the emotional.

I get busy rather than choose to feel; I obsess and ruminate.

Eldest daughter tells me she loves me
in the nighttime car. From nowhere,
she enters an aria:
you have been a good mother,
she says.
What is that?
(Maybe I become a tiny bit
dullard in the asking.)
Dead mother
shimmered when someone
complimented her,
asking *why*
which meant *say more?*

I pity you, she says (who?)(dead mother)(nighttime daughter) continuing the aria. *Because middle daughter will soon attend a school with perfect parents, which must be one percent of the population,* she says, (nighttime daughter) *and middle daughter will contrast you to the perfect.* (No one can do such contrast better than I, however imperfectly.) *But I* (nighttime daughter) *have talked to many people and you are a good mother* (buried mother also said as much in our last colloquy).

What is a good mother? (inner mantra all these years). Since birth, a puzzle with no piece fitting. Surrendering the question never (despite) (because of)(even after): three different daughters.

Pregnant with nighttime-car
daughter, I read
every book on attachment,
the ones my similarly round
friends threw against walls
in disgust at the (impossibility of the) ideal raised:

the all-present parent,
attentive to every need.
If I read enough,
could I understand?
The umbilical Word become Flesh,
transubstantiation
promised by reading and writing
(Roland would agree).

Read enough experts, expect
what you expect, you might get
to become that unknowable mystery:
the good mother.

Donald Winnicott says: please, parents, just be *good enough* and all will work (enough). Tend to needs, don't slay yourself with ideals of perfection, just be present. (Yet ask yourself to be present, you already distance yourself by working at it: the great conundrum.)

Enoughness. Why is it so hard to reach? How driven any of us can be. My grail being to prove (to whom? the ghost of thwarted grandmother? my inner childtime vow?) I could be enough for my children. Be that enough-like parent, you might undo legacy, becoming something other than the great-grandchild of generations lacking the choice of hospitality toward torch-bearers of dispersal, colonization, rape, genocide.

Why am I this
color, I said, sure I was not
of my brown mother.
Rape by Cossacks—my father
laughed, and clear
to me, where mother was concerned,
I may as well have been secretly
adopted.

Be a good mother,
I told myself, as if I existed
enough to be the manipulating
or responding variable
(like you, like any of us)
as if words make intention reality,
as if alchemically you might banish
poison philtered in by all
that trauma induces: *fear,*
flight, freeze,
and our latest, *fawn.*

Around myself,
first gestation of girlchild growing
(and I fawning), Vegas mate just a bit
less livid, ready for this new
version of his being,
I gathered nearby
friends who seemed
to understand motherhood.

One skimmed a careful knife across
the measured teaspoon of baking powder.
Having made warm buttery scones,
she walked the block in
leisurely fashion to give

her brain a vacation; she spoke of walking
with baby. *We like to take walks,* she said,

we the pronoun I never
feel I have the right to use:
the scone-warmed heart(h) of love.

In the kitchen as at the piano,
forever improvising.

Even though *baking—*
our current neighbor,
who happens to be
a joyfully competent biologist
(our avatar of order),
tells my youngest—depends on
(what I lack) chemical exactitude. The youngest is a macaron baker,
she nods, her taste far more exquisite
than my lunches can ever be: our running joke.
She sends a text from school:
dinner you made was delicious last night
and I liked where you were going with lunch today
but it smelled rotten, did you wash
the thermos? Never mind. The secretary
gave me
some of the teachers' lunch. Really don't bother
making lunch tomorrow,
please don't bother
and at home shows me
(the punctum) photos of two
lunches, the one I made an overladen
Soutine disemboweled,
and the neat penne roast vegetable dish
she received
from strangers, as if a gift

from grandfather's long-ago legacy
of charity. Daughter is not homeless
(I protest inside). The contrast of the two photos:
funny because at incongruity
we laugh, and in this case, I
am so far from any ideal,
yet like a clown, I never stop bothering.

Of improvisation I make
an art, yet motherhood
I meant not to invent—
rather, to learn at the feet of the great
mothers. Who were they?
My neighbors? And/or
Sarah? Gaia?
Amina? Bhumi?
Indra? Tara? Teresa?
Waheguru, self-revealing and
necessary, genderless?

Nighttime car drive,
eldest daughter continues
her aria: we are heading
yet again to the patronym,
the house of her father.

She has skidded into eighteen,
that age of self-naming,
having often said I
raised her to be a free-range
mammal, and now resists
the week-on, week-off paradigm
we, divorced, weakly raise
to span rupture:
homes
unpaired.

Collaboration:
Vegas mate and I tried, always
with our burlap
race, our faulty flag
we tried raising at the end
of each goal achieved.

Don't worry, said one angular
curly-haired New Age counselor to all five of us, prior
to the farce of divorce, twinkling ten fingers
near youngest exquisite-taste daughter's face, the one
most prone to taste
hypocrisy or at least falsehood:
you'll have a new constellation of family!

Same grouping, just shaped different
(not saying)
fractured as a mirror, like a spray of lies,
iodine-stung cat-scratches on a girl's leg or face,
seismic faultlines—earthquake!

(Look what you've done to our family,
it is all your fault!
Look how they suffer:
this the intermittent chorus
from the livid and ex.)

A broken home. The cleavage furrow
known by rock and stone.

Geologist's daughter, I seemingly summoned this tectonic plate shift off the Richter scale into being, and for this, I was blamed. Will I one day be forgiven?

Over this fractured earth and into the sky, oldest daughter roams, coordinates unknown. The pact between her friends and me: we text *do you know where she is?*

Where is she?
This daughter in nighttime
car speaks with passion of what
I have done right, saying: *I love you,*
(don't take in the love)
(don't pause)
(never digest). Epigenetic

to the core, instead I rehearse
dread, equip her for war.
I ask if she has
done what she needs to be
ready for the next day
(when torch-bearers might come).

The lesson in my genes:
stack your hay, play
a small violin you can stick
in a satchel when you
must run, be alert to
shift of mood
and tone, be ready to
hide or flee,
find a new home.

Prepare for the worst:
that one has kept
me buried forever: do I now emerge?

What Roland says, emerging from the trauma of his own body forever betraying him, dreaming of roses and attentive lovers, yet frazzled by bouts of tuberculosis: *signs are everywhere.*

Language is a sign for the signified, he says, after Saussure, *and our language exists on a spectrum.* Especially loving to point out the fake binary, always arguing all stern opposition must stay a function of mythology which is really a mask for oppression and tyranny. However, who among us always relishes the joys of the middle way? Is such relishing the destination of adulthood if not enlightenment altogether?

To circumscribe

Early in the time of the great panic, people retreated to their bunkers, though many from the past came forward, and we found a path at a road with a name as if from an early blues song, something like Coffinnail Cove, as if with a line *I'm going out there to find my love.* At the trail-mouth, an older man approached, genial. Hearing of writing, he spoke of his own. No longer did he care for home construction, his business card's first metier, he cared for spreading his name out on the waters. Skeptical about the invisible glittervirus, he tried palming the card directly into beau's hand, as the little rectangle also mentioned his first or last book. His wife stood by, similarly skeptical about his need to have this recent construction, the writing self, recognized.

With care, we placed his card between two rocks for later retrieval, so it would not moulder too quickly, and returned to this east coast forest, so splendid in its understanding of all collaboration with death and memento mori. Branches fell earthward only to climb upward from new roots. And inside one hollowed trunk, on a moss-covered pelt, a bark-prince sat, coolly regarding all hubris, our ideas about forward motion.

Brief lecture on semiology

Offered last night to an island-mate who asked, a cheery Dutchwoman photographer with big wonderful hands:

that, according to Roland, even your gestures, even your shirt, is a *sign* which represents. Each sign has two meanings: denotative or connotative. We organize denotations and connotations into myth which make ideology natural. Our assumption of such ideology as universal—our tendency to accept myth sans nuance or differentiation—blinds us.

Take the denotation of *egg*. Call it whatever you want, organic matter, proteins with a palisade layer of crystalline calcium carbonate columns, a container holding the embryo of a future bird. The connotation of an egg, as Roland and others would have it, would be our thoughts or feelings associated with cyclicity, purity, hope, spring ritual, renewal, a dream of flight, something to be tended and warmed.

He goes on about denotations signifying connotations. Sometimes the connotative field alters, losing historic meaning, just because an event, culture, history, or terminology shifts. Say someone ripped away the idea of free-range or Petaluma's bolshevist poultry farmers, say there were no halal egg or golden egg for Prajapati, no cupola in a stupa, no Easter hunting or Passover plating: what then happens to an egg's meaning?

From the above, he limns a greater truth: all of us live on a wavelength, depending on how *motivated* our speech and actions are by social codes. His goal is that we stay attuned to how every act—including every speech-act—lives as a little mushroom nub peeking up from a giant greater subterranean fungus of cultural, ideological, and hence mythical meaning.

And so you can find that Roland ends up a grapher of chaos, seeing a nullity at the heart, a sort of blissful emptiness. And might also note that he believes in an artwork which calls overt attention to the form and fact of its fabrication. For him, only certain acts have any true residue of the *natural*: obvious moments of your animal life, such as when you are born, eat, sleep, have sex, die. Other moments stay wed to connotation and hence myth and ideology.

A dead father's hat may live as your hands torture it. Your senses may know the hat (punch it, stroke it, crush it), yet the hat also participates in greater cultural ideas you have about fatherhood or death, and this is what Roland calls the *abstract* connection of a sign to its meaning.

While Roland says some signs or symbols may be even more tightly *motivated*. Say your father casually finds and brings home an American cop's cap from two decades ago. The thing that sits as a quiet object on a doorstand cannot be understood apart from its operations: U.S. history, lineage, racism, sexism, patriarchy, oppression. The most tyrannical systems will blur the individual into the collective, the essence into the individual, and such myth exists everywhere.

In this light, Roland calls some signs so motivated they are what he calls *driven*: the sign almost disappears and merges wholly with the signified. If we were to invent now this symbol—%— as a means of telling the story of the cap from two decades ago, we would encounter what he calls the driven. When the thinnest system conveys the grandest, tightest scheme, you will find the least movement or variability, the least individual movement or autonomy.

Each sign also tries to make itself understood in different ways. *Symbolic* (the color red can represent passion); *paradigmatic* (red is not green, it is understood by what it negates); the *syntagmatic* (red can function as an analogy—it operates within the rainbow, within the history of color, up and down and across your memory and the question of collective perception).

The Dutch photographer with the wonderful hands clapped, nodding inside our mossfairy forest. For the moment quiet but not lacking in interest. Once I began talking of Roland, I sometimes could not stop myself. Yet in our forest I felt the great void at the end of any string of words, as if at the close of analysis: together we shared an interest, but why did I think any of this mattered?

What is the myth that matters to you? the photographer asked.

Being a good-enough mother. That's my real one.

She had chosen not to have kids and understood.

That's why I convinced my last man we were not fit to have kids.

But what about art? Isn't art also a myth? She may not have known I had no exact clue, but her great laugh let the question drop.

The good mother. Such myth—I could have told the photographer—that one can garrote your throat the way a wedding ring can grow too tight.

You who are parents, do not let it choke you. Abstract concept, motivated and driven, symbolic or syntagmatic, yes, but the concept of the good mother can almost kill those who are epigenetic self-improvers. All myth plays all the time at being natural.

In this case, this particular myth stuffs my ears, occluding the possibility of my hearing any news daughter ever shared with me about being good for her, except that I write her nighttime car homage and aria here, o code of literature, an epitaph of words tall and mythologizing against other winds.

We are our own demons

Prevailing winds in college: every one of my professors had been overinfluenced by Roland (egg-eater, card-keeper, shadow-lover, mother loyalist, pirouette artist). I took all of three Shakespeare classes, each time dreaming of peering deeply into mystery, each time disappointed by Roland-laden guides, disillusion and tricksters themselves great Shakespearean themes. For thirteen weeks, one professor's major point: the letter O remained the focus of the story of Othello—

—and going deeper, the O was the stage, proscenium arch, and shape of an Elizabethan theater in its entirety, yet also was the O of absence and implication: what you fill in with novelty, anxiety, pleasure, meaning. O! Consider the story: Othello's jealous Iago invents an empty O of a story implicating Othello's appointee Cassio, saying Cassio made the beast with two backs with Othello's own wife Desdemona. The whole plot an O, O becoming the space in which nothing exists and into which everything can flow.

Thus this O oriented the offering I had hoped would be such an opening of that semester. Nothing filled our guide's oratory other than O, and yet in it started one of the greatest overtures of my life: a lifelong friendship with a queer man who offered such open love and recognition, I could name my own habit of nonconformity. The refuge of wearing father's over-large shirts. Why dressing female stayed a drag borrowed from a mother whose own femininity had been a kind of anachronism, a switched-era drag.

Sweetheart, so obvious, you are the first young woman I have met so much like me—just another gay man in a woman's body. This said by my first true boss after my semester of Os: in Los Angeles, a palm-laden high-glassed restaurant, her live pet rat on her shoulder. Who was she? A woman with a great shiny bald head. Wistful, gracious, insightful, no-holds-barred, ministerial, charismatic, lower-chakra-bawling, Paris-accented animal activist and grande dame of performance art, the long-ago daughter of a pearl king, the former wife of the first McDonald's clown, then an ecological pioneer who had also been third-wheel friend to the great gay couples of Manhattoes, Cunningham and Cage, Rauschenberg and Johns.

Gay man inside a woman's body. My destiny she named, offering a gift I then lost in all later years' moves, as well as a felt hat from an old-style hatbox. *Can you not see?* She wished me to be clear. She cared for clarity. Around this tall bald prophet flocked a bevy of ex-Mormons, wraiths and bears, artists queering performance, my main colleague a young boy who had played assistant to pop divas, punctilious about wiping down computer keys.

Please, she said, *your first task is to see yourself.* Every young person should have guides, yet how easy to be obstinate in listening. And yet still wisdom pokes through. Easy to understand why putting on eyeliner as if to soften twitchy Los Angeles traffic cops (stagey legacy of mother) had always felt as if it were the greatest drag. Or why I may have loved songs with antiheroines named Lola, Jane, Candy. Or followed films about vagabonds, people ruined by sympathy, held hostage, angels fallen to earth. Roland says: *the professionalism of the striptease artist keeps her cloaked. The angles of the movie star's face hide her.*

Consider you too may have been born natural and quickly grew into imposter syndrome (myth). Childhood has so many steppingstones, so much learning and bliss, but so many stones are the same: shame and its opposite, awe. The word of one's innermost self gets misunderstood and society, prematurely or not, offers us gender and sexuality. Should there not be one long word for that slow process of misunderstanding? Is it partly to be found in the invisible ink between these lines?

The calendar transformed

O, consider this game. What if we each kept a true calendar which marked every anniversary of the firsts, each serpent swallowing its own tail, the O of loss or gain?

Each date can be a proscenium, a hollow stage now yet also, bear with me, a palimpsest. An O-shaped stone: memory laid over by the deepest carving or most recent rubbing.

One evening, July third, I plunged into new intimacy with the man who later became Vegas mate. That afternoon, a defense against hunger, I had been trying to set him up with another woman.

Future Vegas mate had arrived in California to visit someone down the coast. That morning, I picked him up—as a friend—at the San Francisco airport.

A brief affair with X years earlier, followed by my hosting that preferred game on the isle of Manhattoes: a whimsical party specked by *what do you do?* a favorite amid a herd of workaholics in their twenties. (How can a workaholic be present for anyone else?) Prescient or not, I made a short silent film starring future Vegas mate, its plot made of a later game: his failure to notice the woman before him who kept becoming someone else.

During that period, I worked three service jobs, running around the city, yet because I had been with so many older than I, it seemed best to avoid anyone not my age. Much farther into the future, once I linked with Vegas mate, seventeen years older, a wise friend joked: you're cradle-robbing!

All around me, the isle's tournament startled: people seemed to keep dropping to marriage. Ambitious women not quite my direct friends read secret rule-cards unaddressed to me about what it means to approach thirty.

Instead, for fun, I kept organizing big picnics along the Hudson River, near the tiny shiproom I rented on the Upper West Side, offering up platters of delicacies and also future Vegas mate, introducing him to some potential person or another. One wild-haired Lizzy demanded: what's the bad about him?

Funny, alive, passionate, good values, I said, along with some other notes. And so kept him in that status—the ex/friend. He would leave long voice messages in which he perhaps seemed a bit stuck in the past, ruing mistakes made with ex-girlfriends.

But July third, fateful day, he came to visit some old friend on the west coast. I picked him up in the San Francisco airport and without preamble, at baggage claim, he blurted *would you have my children?*

Baggage claim! Because saving can be my great compulsion, I had asked my mother to organize a dance party: my mother would snake her arms and ding zils with her friends and he might meet someone.

At the midpoint of her life, my mother had begun to teach dance on the side. This came from a suggestion given by Fawn, the California guru-like figure who was at various points in my late childhood my father's secretary, our live-in family/couple's therapist, a crucial director and savior of so many lives including my own.

This bellydance teaching meant that most Sundays saw an influx of women to our home, to the same mirrored room in which my mother would die two decades hence, women carrying colored scarves and finger cymbals. (My mother talking about the happy inhabitation of women in their bodies: *the art form began as female-to-female sensuality,* she said, deemphasizing that it began as a way to help others in labor.) *I never had problems with female stuff,* she liked telling me privately, another drag dominion over any betrayal by the female body.

Shall we have a party of bellydancers? The nighttime would unroll in that fine rich-toned cluttered but gemütlich living room which had seen so many parties, the ladies coming out and gyrating or sometimes obscenely thrusting as if at a rock concert, not understanding the discretion and history of the form, though reminded by my mother's carmine lips pursing, as she had learned well from her Egyptian teacher about constraining flirtation, necessary limits.

In laying out platters on the jewel-toned tablecloth, it became obvious that I should match future Vegas mate with one particular dancer, R, a Fawn student and family friend who would this last year help play overture for the death march of mother's belongings.

Toward evening, R passed future Vegas mate and me at the foot of the orange-carpeted stairs of childhood home, prancing upward toward the deep lemon-musk-and-jangly-armor-necklace land of mother still putting on her face for the later dance performance during which she would make a grand entrance. Not-yet-husband and I shared the trance of watching R from below. Have I mentioned matchmaking intent? He threw a comment up the stairs. From the landing, R tossed down a sassier joke. That slight ping of jealousy let me know I cared. If not for whatever happened between Vegas mate and me later that evening, the two of them might have ended up together, and I with another marriage and epigenetic history for my children.

Sleeping in Uncle Rick's room, he was, walls newly painted hunting-lodge green: no place I wished to reenter. Yet after the party I came to hug him goodnight, and was it the coziness of that house or the molecules of that exact second or some tricky signifier which predicted welcome change? A glow of well-being. What slippery augury: we would decidedly lack hygge. In the bond's unhitching, I ended up deported from whatever home he and I had aimed to create, multigravida, leading to these last years of seeking new refuge.

So why, that July third, did I orient toward him? See another and recognition warms—is that destiny? What imago delights you? The lessons you are supposed to learn. Juggle intimacy and autonomy your whole life, a great circus act, precariously tightrope some destiny, and then stumble into believing you find right land.

Another July third, in Vegas, we joined in eyes of law and friends on the eve of the day of independence, according to the US of A. I walked around him seven times, already knowing his livid rage: did I dissociate? Did the light of nearby candles keep us flushed and close? Was this the right choice?

Sassy R took photos of our wedding, which she had also helped organize, gently shoving three of our living parents down the nubbly carpeted aisle.

And in California this past year of the float, R also became executor of my mother's will until she smartly shucked the task, another sassy joke sent downstairs.

The orange-carpeted stairs murderously stripped this last month—

stripped, to the great sadness of mother's last true witness in California, grotto tenant, who said some team must have been hired for two hundred a day—the phrase sticks in my mind—to fling down the fifty-one stone stairs outside, in tied black garbage bags, all the objects accrued over a lifetime of gentle Depression-era, peasant-mind hoarding. Glass crashing, cacophony.

The tenant's email quivered with outrage: the objects of a lifetime, no dignity!

The last witness to her realm whom I have admired for his stripped-down way of life.

This basement tenant had named his home the grotto. People living the fiercely curated life can seem as if they understand choice, control, and how to have a greater lease on happiness. He lived among four surfboards, three bikes, his weekly service in a food pantry, his blithe thirty-hour-a-week tech talent and the half-time presence of a lovely mellow mate. His good cheer came from all he had eschewed, a message I would soon try to heed. Yet he had not begun the process of divorcing a long-ago wife. Having fathered his one daughter, he had his circle-of-ten friends for whom he would do anything. Some people have an a priori plan, and but for the unstarted divorce, the tenant lived well inside chosen pillars, believing in no afterlife: such could make a person more present.

Together he and I would coordinate emergency-room visits and brainstorm helping my mother whenever Uncle Rick vanished. I would fly to California and the tenant and I met so often over mother's swollen empurpled toes. How wondrously happy she could be in those hospital rooms, treating each person as a gracious visitor. Her loyal writing group came and she would be there, bubbling and hissing away with walrus-like oxygen tubes inserted in her nose, a diver into the depths of mortality, even though before their arrival, she wanted life's full drag: her hair and lipstick done, she beamed at her circle of ten as they earnestly wrote with such devotion.

Their work she had produced and put on as plays for years, and they loved what she had released in them: *the most creative moments of my life have been because of her.* She had evolved a format, being a dedicated student of the form of creative-writing practice—such as it exists—offering them a photograph Roland would have loved toward which they would write, and then exhorting them to recall their favorite moments from the others' read-aloud work.

The first time I came to be a guest teacher for her—she called it, for her writers, a master class—I was struck by the consumption, not of words but of California delicacies: garlic crackers, morels, overstuffed olives, veined cheese. Their chomping a scritchy ASMR track that accompanied the scratching on paper tablets. For thirty years, her writers met as a group, crunching, shifting, adopting new members and mores, so that around her hospital bed, they lovingly accepted the failing of her form, having learned their greatest lesson from her, that anyone's content mattered far less than community.

Who were they? Art-adjacent bruised Californians trying to live lives of meaning in between meeting friends for hikes in fire-brushed hills. *The great problem* Roland says in one of his later conversations *is to outplay the signified, to outplay law, to outplay the father, to outplay the repressed—I do not say to explode it, but to outplay it.* Her students played and she with them. Together they became one another's ideal readers, a tail-biting serpent, ouroboros.

Everyone arrives in California gripping strong ideas. I met my future X inside the airport so I could bring him toward my hometown and its power, kundalini, melding, deep-rooted oaks, fire, quakes; the phrasing of his baggage-claim question now seems crucial. Could Roland parse X's question enough to see how the ancient code of family outplayed me? Alternating days of storm and calm, X managed to nudge each member of extended family and finally me out of our home. There on that first July third, at baggage claim, his joke would be made unfunny only by later years: *would you have* my *children?*

In the worst of times, X would talk with his enfeebled croupier father, now a self-appointed pawnbroker, who always tried thrusting on X one particular book which would explain females to his son so he would not be a *freier*, the word for sucker.

What was the title of this book?

The Biological Tragedy of Womanhood and does that matter now? Has ever a sign been more linked to its signified, so tightly wound? Handing over the book to his son as if a gesture of benevolence: the fantastic symmetry of the mirror. Even non-narcissists need complements. With such a book, father believed, son and I might ascend to the highest heavens of coupledom.

And the oddity of our collective post-ripcord years rests in how memories twist. Who among us has not been thrust out of our past as much as shut within? Homes taken apart and reconstituted and we within them. Years with an infinite replication of pattern mirrored within us all. How can anyone then speak the same tongue?

A story: youngest daughter, the baker, stands with me in line. We have decided finally to get her excellent bread. Joyful or depressed farmers and back-to-the-landers from nearby join each Saturday in an outdoor market to offer goods to those who flee rough cities. Anyone at the market is living out some version of Alcott's utopia, the gentry-farmer dream of self-subsistence: freedom from vertical steel-plated tragedy wrought by others' greed.

Daughter and I stand in line. The seller, a young woman in shades, her plank bearing four loaves of bread, begins using a loudly enunciated nonviolent dialect with a man in similar shades, her customer: *please step back from the stand. I do not feel safe, I am not feeling comfortable with you. When you speak, I feel uncomfortable.* The man is angry, pressing close, he wants an answer to the question. *Why are you selling twelve-dollar loaves? How do we know that money goes toward charity? It's highway robbery! What portion of it goes to charity?* His rage that of a frustrated idealist. *I'm a reporter, this is fraud, how do you get away with selling twelve-dollar loaves?*

What is poor communication? When each treats the other as an object to be managed. When both want to be treated as human, with human needs that can be heard. While his ire is inappropriate, her professionally correct handling of him escalates it, or at least so my survivor's ear hears.

With another bystander, well-coiffed yet of the fellow compulsive-savior variety, I try to help, and yet the aggressor's hand grips a tall push-cart: red iron, a heraldic shield of the sort X's father used to use. The aggressor will not budge; the bystander and I ask the seller if she wants us to watch her stuff as she looks to find security. The problem (Roland or Bakhtin would appreciate) is that no carnival ever possesses adequate security: what adult is there to protect us? No overwatching eye can save moments in which humans play out Babel's curse, refusing to speak the same tongue.

Having been assaulted too many times, I understand both why the seller cloaked herself in automated response and also how the choice irritated the man. Is it sad that all my years with X teach me to understand exactly why clarity can inflame?

Finally a moment opens, a wrinkle in time, and the pushcart man leaves with the paltriest assurance of his rightness, poisoned ether around us all. *What just happened?* Youngest daughter, the baker, wants me to explain. What can be said? The man's rage masked his wound; the seller's hurt covered her anger; neither found middle ground. That dream of a common language—I still hold it, wishing to be some kind of interpreter. No failure; all is seemingly resolved.

Yet when I recall all the times in marriage I drove to cry alone in cold dark parking lots far from children, sluicing through ice puddles, I wonder what perseverance made me think a certain dialect could help us or why strength fled me: why could I not also flee the dynamic of our arguments? (I kept dreaming of resolution.) Could we not have seen far earlier that the terrible content, the nouns, did not matter? Could we not have ended the thing or, conversely, just focused on peace as love? So easy to see mistakes in hindsight. How easily we fell prey to some curse, Babel or not, believing the spells of pogrom-accented ghosts.

When your mind spirals, it takes great lifeblood just to meditate, say, to imagine a simple black dot—the finality of a period, or death. To englobe what seems so inconstant in this time of people not breathing, whether from illness biological or societal. The O of absence, the betrayal of nothingness, the everything lack can contain. Your mind races rather than finds its home.

That first July third, on the way to my childhood home from the airport, surprisingly, future Vegas mate lay his head in my lap as if a child. At a gas station, he made a big show of squeegee-washing the car windows as I sat inside, making a funny joke out of hard labor. The lineaments of all later relationship are revealed in the first week: his joke of selfhood minus work. I ended up working too hard and he, at home, refused or was ejected from so many jobs or chose his urgent substitute truck-driving.

But how hard we linked in our devotion to one myth. We wished to be that thing, *the devoted father and mother*, the drag every parent puts on at first conception of the ideal. Our constant slide up and down the spectrum of conventional gender assignment. Father and mother. Who can help anyone now? O we parents are glad for the children. O we lost the battles but gained the beauty of knowing these gifts. These children. O there is never true hindsight but can a new view open? O please.

Hot flash/the unknowable

Roland says *the absence of the other holds my head underwater; gradually I drown, my air supply gives out; it is by this asphyxia that I reconstitute my 'truth' and that I prepare what in love is Intractable.*

If your body shifts enough, maybe the religious
affections of the world might be restored.

You might begin to know what it means if a goddess rises
from grove gorge,
overheated, invoked:

in this case, your new love strokes your hand, the flush
untied unto greater truth.

You thought you were alone but the earth came searching after you as a mother
after a child, all you can do is rest until stilled

breeze returns. *The heart is what I imagine I give. It is not true*
that the more you love, the better you understand; all that

the action of love obtains from me is merely this wisdom: that the other
is not to be known; his opacity is not a screen around the secret.

I am then seized with that exaltation of loving someone unknown, someone
who will remain so forever, a mystic impulse: I know what I do not know.

Youngest daughter has made
a beautiful bouquet gift,
an offering: dried wildflowers
(no starfish)
falling from the pages
of your favorite Roland book
in that glade suffused with heat:

could you not feel all is right
(enough)
with the world
this exact beat?

Atopos

Here, back east,
I keep seeing wrong
things in the right places, howling
faces everywhere but
especially in the upturned
roots: great fallen trees,
guts entombed in mud.

There is no change of death in Paradise, says Wallace, enshrined in Hartford, one hour south of where I usually live in the newish parsonage, but he might as well have been schrying California.

Might as well have said *there is no change of Paradise in death:* your horizon of hope after a beloved dies may not alter.

A kind of epic without the heroic, Roland says of Maman, mourning her lifelong struggles, and also: *what I find terrifying is mourning's discontinuity.* Rupture of a rupture: who loves that?

What becomes a binary best: do we most trust what stays?

Or do we least trust what might rupture?

What if we only know how to trust when ruptured?

The whole time I grip on to the ideal of motherhood
it seems to be happening without
my noticing, around me, in the cracks.

Anxiety

Roland's mother, cast out of her own mother's fancy family, makes do in the bosom of the less cultured family of her late husband. Young Roland clings to her: large, at the age where he is *meant to be* standing alone.

What would Donald Winnicott say? Henrietta was more than a good-enough mother. Present if querulous. As Roland says, days after her death: *I keep hearing her voice telling me to wear a little color.*

Meant to be: a young man standing on spindly legs facing the photographer. Instead, he clings, watchful, big for his shorts, the distance between the two mandated. The question remains: would he suckle if he could?

Wouldn't anyone? Middle daughter says she cannot help the jealousy, seeing me hold someone's flirtatious baby: *I miss that belonging to you,* she says, *I want to be a baby all over.* Knowing herself that much.

Later I intone, pedantic: all war comes from the same wish: if not to suckle then to belong! Everyone covers the wish to belong and connect. They feel hurt and over that lay in the mud of righteousness, uproar, spleen, identity, tribalism, the martial.

You should be a daily influencer, she says, *I subscribe to stuff like that, it helps me survive, I'd subscribe to you,* and in what she says I flush with belonging, feeling I belong not just to her but to the umbilicus of outermost signs, the screen a transitional object, that I might yet become the mother-screen she thumbs and believes.

After the photo, Roland goes on to live with mother on and off for some fifty years, seeing her struggles as noble. Friends and foes will call him an avid, rapacious guest at their dinner parties, a man eternally legislating the discord between body and mind, on diet plans meant to contain the wish: to suckle more than he needs. His body continues the great betrayal begun in adolescence: at the sanatorium instead of college, breathing afresh an institution's order, its community and meals. Hypervigilant and frail within traitorous body, he micro-analyzes what happens on the surface of his villi and skin, attends costume galas in broad swashbuckling drag.

Chère Maman cheers from the sidelines, and back home, he makes up for lost time, lives with her. For a half-century! (She dies.) A handful of months beyond her death, in a fug, he is hit by a laundry truck and soon follows that originating body, mother, tunnels down toward her, and will no longer be betrayed by the waxwork of physical self, the question worn by coming out of her. He melts back toward the woman who offered him ressentiment, whose worth he believed had never been fully understood, high-born but treated wrongly by her own motherroot. Having explicated the worth of the individual and her choices, the slippery code of the self as it struggled to communicate such worth to anyone who would understand. A boy born second year of the first world war in the same era that one poet declaimed *the center could not hold* and another called out to a chorus of angels and asked could anyone hear? The world falling apart birthed the question: what private voice can be heard and understood? Forget mother—might understanding itself become a lover, with unmothering only the background, a world-echo?

Attentive

Then Jonathan
said to David tomorrow
is the new moon, and you
will be missed, because
your seat will be empty.

A brief history of love,
genus solipsistic: as a child, my first
memory of mother (is it
possible?), eight months of age:

Toronto where she had been
hired to be a biologist
in an era when women never
were such things! Baby recall:
narrow womblike corridor
toward a gold-bling chain:
a security latch. A blast of cold.

Later, ocher Los Angeles
pale light fluttering curtains,
a short broad window
seen through eternal time spent
in wood-slatted cage,
older brother in nearby crib.
At the stove,
a hired ambivalent Scotswoman,
manic-depressive, raised
in an orphanage, unwitty
in combing hair harshly as
had been done to her.

Looking across a kitchen, under
five, at someone else: who?

Mother. Watching that alluring
dark-haired lipsticked
stranger called
mommy:
she was making a sandwich.
Might I go toward her?
No. I barely knew what to call the stranger.
She worked; wanted
a doctorate not a daughter,
neither award nor diploma
to be found
in the boiling of diapers.

Other uncertain caretakers surfaced:
the rule being I should charm and
attach to each before, months
later, they left, unreachable.

Bullies and others flowed
in to fill the vacuum, their refined
habit. No refuge in
the house not a home.
Heart's message: *be loved*
for doing, not being;
charm or be left! Protect or flee!

Alteration

At readings, people would ask: *why so much focus on Roland?* I'd say: do you prefer an answer from feminist film theory or autobiography?

The canon taught me to develop a particular gaze in which the desired one is female while power accrues to the male. And then suggested I see women as my father did: attractive shills, deep reflecting ponds, lyric muses skilled at bringing out father's aqueous poet soul.

Animus, anima, like many, I began to read, think, and write as a man. (To do so meant to leave the home of sadness and get to travel.) In a way I could not recognize (instead)(for all these reasons)(before my bald boss and her decree) I identified privately: a gay man in a woman's body.

Consider that first obvious coming-of-age moment, bat mitzvah age thirteen on the ides of March, the aleatory wisdom in being assigned singsong chants off an ancient burnt scroll hidden from spilled blood: the rich story of David and Jonathan, those boys entwined in fields, plotting the world before knowing its cost.

With both that king's son and his lovely interloper, at thirteen I identified, though how does the signified walk into the world? Such deep longing lived in my gullet: that my brother might receive for once an approving hug from my father. Same-sex friendship a totem to be guarded. Let David and Jonathan not be sundered, let Ruth glean for Naomi.

And the nearby San Francisco pageant did not clarify much: Castro cops, cowboys, sailors, the signified swallowing sign, like the Mapplethorpe billboards of that time, white and black men staring out as if to dare, the hearty Oakland lesbians in low-slung jeans and their heroines in overalls on album covers.

In library-dusted hands, great women writers of my time and earlier passed through, but never did I dream you get to choose as career what you love. Instead I thought to become (like mother) a scientist: observe the world in humility and report findings, not yet realizing this was the same code you might crack by reading or writing. The paradox of solipsism turned outward: Roland's core theme.

If ever I dared write, I believed, best to publish under a male pseudonym. Because under a name no one knows, you find sanctuary from bullies. (And once I did publish, some rascals from my past came forth, offering that most asymmetrical text, the dream of a common language, an apology.) A new name might let a person doff all girlhood's cost, risk, and vulnerability, in the spirit of Edward Said, who calls the final stage of a nation coming into awareness the invention of its own undone name.

Contingencies

That era: men
falling in the streets of
San Francisco. That era
in college: meaningful nighttimes
of gay antidefamation dances
(mother, where are you?).
That alluring dark-haired
lesbian dancing nearby.

That era: the lifetime friend I met,
light shining from behind his head
at the Providence station.
What grace.
Over the ricketing clatter
of the train, that new friend
with whom I spoke
for seven hours, asking
training-wheel questions
about homosexuality.

Before, during, after: I met
people, was with them, lived
with them. I slept, sidled,
was touched. And yet inside
forever kept safe the
sanctum sanctorum
and mantram of (my) love:
never trust. Cauterized feeling. Soul
and epigenetic song of that time:
leave.

Lost to the dust of
history. Who in the rising
seas will care what
is acted, said, written? What forest
can be planted
to redeem these leaves?
The poisoned bugs amass
because of the morass we have made.

Festivity

That era: my mother!
She came to see my
value when I returned home with a fancy
college degree and became a person
of interest.
On a monthly basis, she
hired me to help her pursue
creativity.

On a hunch, worried myself
(rehearsing dread,
wishing not to repeat mistakes,
to have an unwanted child), I asked her:
was I a mistake? It turned out,
yes, I was: horror
at the news of me, Ivory soap
the old-time contraceptive.
There in her big new job,
designing experiments in Toronto!

To be saddled with another kid—
who wanted me?
No one, not then.

As the genius friend says:
Now I understand!
You were never met
by that good-enough motherly
effusive adoration.

Rather, young,
I knew myself first as
a burden: wishing to earn

my keep, feeling
myself the maid
rising at five to bake and offer each sleeper
blueberry muffins as I did, understanding
early that unlove of love: performance.

To hide

Roland, do you understand? I didn't know maman until I was twenty-one. I take myself to task for not having shared more. *We should go out some time,* she kept saying to my adult self, *to lunch!* As if a novel concept. Beyond the blueberry muffin: we might share a meal.

And by the end we came to know each other: respect, love, closure—is that not enough to heal all?

She too lived with ambivalent attachment. One Valentine's Day in Oakland toward the end of my father's life, to him she read a reproachful poem against love. At a freighted table in the low-rent penthouse apartment where I lived with the man twenty-seven years older as if a second mother, my first read her anti-love poem, ending in a cataclysm: *Once I needed you, husband, I thought you were a god, now I do not* (a song of emancipation).

Who was my father? He perfected the art of sitting as a stone statue, face unmoving during and after dramatic pieces my mother performed about people for whom she may have longed. An era both looser and yet less expressive. Father sat through performances that splayed public revenge against his own hunger for the soulful lyric muse to be found in others. *What did you think?* (I once asked his military posture and Lincoln face).

I thought
I thought
I thought
she gave a very good performance tonight, he said, recovering himself,
forever skewing toward the picturesque, the positive.

But there is proof of attachment, some love documents, *true writing* as Roland would say—not what he would call *écriture*, the official writing of, say, that of a state tyrant who might mention a lakeside forest in order to control his citizens' identity. Notes mother wrote in her own style, offering a metaphoric lake that asked nothing of me: loving notes she sent whenever I was frequently shipped off outside the home, to camp or anywhere. Did she not (in her way, with her art) tend me?

Consider the home she provided, rituals of caring and structure. Can rituals of a home not be enough?

Induction

Can't you just become an insurance agent?
she said (to me at twenty-three)
when on the isle of Manhattoes
I dreamed of burning
a gemlike fire
like that notorious
neighbor, the satyr male
writer, whose nighttime
light and discipline never
went out, the one whose sexist
eros she admired
until his death
preceded hers.

And yet: the warm
grandmother she became to
my daughters. Her baby
talk when applying thick white
stripes of diaper paste.
Her love of buying
matching pajamas.
From where had such mother
instinct appeared?

Her last time with me, I testify,
she came to see me
as if for the first time.

What does it mean to feel
seen by your mother?
Delicious beyond all earth.
There is no change of death
in Paradise.

Reader, do you care? Were you seen by a parent? Does it matter when people are dying in deserts and oceans, roofless, bearing tarp and leaky canteens?

But to know mother's love—*mother is Mother,* as a well-loved taxi driver once informed me—at least once, if you got that much, that at least once you were seen, that fact never dies.

Our moment: *you are so good and kind* (she said, fingering my unbroken rose quartz on a chain) *and generous and caring, yet you like simple things like this necklace. I like how you are so simple. My children are simple.* The thought comforted her enough to return to troubled medicated sleep.

So bright and loving from the hospital bed rigged in her mirrored home studio, in the house she kept going for all of us, a shiplike creature run by bo'suns and others, a seemingly permanent landing-place for grandchildren. With my own breath bated—out of the fog of meds my mother emerged.

Rose quartz (say the California mystics) *the great heart protector.*

Out east, just a few weeks later, the stone broke on the floor, hours before I heard of her death. I wear it still: better to wear the rough than never have had it at all. Her love at the end and the stone, its surface corrugated like her words and the latterday sight we had of each other: can you understand how the rough can mean the world?

As the divorce began to break and spread over the waters like an oily mess, the gift of childhood abandonment fear which made me seek only the ultra-loyalists, she was already on her way out.

Annulment

Most often these giant roots look like ganglia under consideration.

Take this as a first premise: we begin with fear. Your amygdala might most easily recall all the times in your life you have been hauled out of whatever is safe and comfortable, and then were able to find a perch you believed safe: at least that seems the message of our forest.

Some of the thicket: three daughters depend on me and a book I meant to write for which I hocked the family fortune, piddling as it may be, nest egg socked away during years of the long marriage which last year (I/he/they/we) ended.

Imagine this simple hope: borrow from one future to write a book of the past.

A book which might cover nothing less than time, memory, coupling, the whole universe of love, even though I am only learning about it now.

A book for which an underpaid publicist had to send a catalog description long before the thing was writ:

A riveting and engrossing read on Roland Barthes destined to change the very nature of reading itself, to shed light on gender relations, tribal misprision, national legacy, coupling, mothers, divorce, illness, death, love, light, ecological crisis, immigrant rights, regeneration, and all the rest of our puzzle.

That one figure stood at the head of this parade, twiddling his baton, ready to be put to use, the man on whom I had rested my entire career, such as it is, ever since I was a waitress who kept getting fired for my face that telegraphed much too quickly.

My sign: symbol, paradigm, a little too syntagmatic.

Back in Los Angeles after college: either as a waitress I chatted too much with the funny, other-directed clientele or (apparently) once/finally showed horror: the famous scary-film producer! A short man treating his smart mate as if he had invented the word *bimbo*, as if he owned her and more. *Sorry, you're being put on furlough,* said the manager right after to me, deferentially at the coffee station, a dark corridor with its musk of spilled beer, where creamers stacked more neatly than the future that seemed might be mine, white witnesses watching me understand this first of my (long line of) waitress firings!

I listened to both sign and signified of that (melancholic blond-handlebarred former Kinsey sex researcher) manager:

The owner thinks you don't like certain customers, here's your last check, what's your hurry, we always seemed to like each other.

What is it to show liking? You can (fail to) show affinity in so many ways; or you can believe in someone who gets that the understanding of likeness has everything to do with the greater codes and forces running through all of us.

As a waitress soon to be fired
three times, I could not put myself
on furlough. Turning off the
sign of my face: this
among many challenges
Roland could have helped.
Some photographs he called
a message without a code,
yet I felt much the same in life: codeless.
If my goal was to write
on Roland, I
lived equipped only
with the uncertainty of his principles.
In front of the lens, I am at the same time: the one

I think I am, the one I want others
to think I am, the one the photographer
thinks I am, and the one
he makes use of to exhibit his art.

Mad

True urban legend: a con
artist perpetrated
a twenty-year
-long fraud on lonely
men by speaking as
a woman to thousands
in xeroxed letters. He had
a computer fill text-fields with
personal names—
to Bob, Rick, Bill, Jeff, Ryan—
all signed by angel
Pamela or Vanessa.
The con man's
gift: brilliance in reflecting others'
wounds of narcissism.

This particular trick
seemed key to survival in
my early years. *People like us*
see the good in life, darling,
the con artist would say,
people like us want to care and love.

To love is to want
to belong to the realm of
people like us.
If you speak right,
maybe you find that
exact bridge
between longing and
belonging.

The con artist spoke
in sympathy
with his demographic (lonely
older men), saying, essentially: *you are*
like me. Your innards are no
different than mine.
I recognize how you began
and now choose to
operate within the universe.
We like each other.

Oddest: once the con
was revealed, the artist confronted,
the men turned
angry, yes, about being
fooled, but stayed wistful:
yearning still for the
(writer as con artist)
one who had seemed
to recognize (uniquely) them.

Catastrophe

So, my father said, some months before, *you're going to graduate from your fancy school and be a waitress in Los Angeles?* We stood like awkward ibex shunted to the side of what he believed was my college graduation.

Okay, fine, I'd understand if you were the manager or owner sorry *but waitress* sorry, yes. He didn't like the choice; he felt no affinity, it made no sense to his cosmogony. We were not alike. The prole intelligentsia might make some sense but I failed the family's religion: a workaholic, fine, but retreat a generation in class?

You don't care you'll end up with your brain bored not sure *so what, your highest hope to write about your Roland and splash a little paint on canvases and take photos* yes *so you can become—what, a waitress with a fancy degree* yes *or what's that called, a sonographer or tutor like what's-his-face's kid, what's that called, a doula, a masseuse* I don't know *selling vegetables at the farmer's market like that pregnant girl from your school who was a drug addict or what, a chiropractor?* Really not sure no exact plans *you got to think about your* choices anything but *your hands will be there cracking spines in the afternoon* is that the end of the world? *but your brain will be bored. What will you be thinking* freedom from the brain *catching babies?* Autonomy.

My father never knew the babies well. Vita interrupta. He stopped reading my first monograph on Roland after the epigraph. He died before I got to answer any bunch of things.

For one, consider this deadlock: I never truly graduated from that fancy school. Sign, symbol, syntagm snarled in my performance.

During the actual ceremony, mother east of the field, father westerly, I lurked south, as if we were forever a family destined to hold down the points of the flyaway parachute meant to save us.

What I held: a heavy giant spattered tempera-on-cardboard puppet, its mouth an eternal paroxysm, an O. All the other students, some sincere, useful activists and others like me just in the moment's flummery, continued marching north toward the dais with huge processional puppets, protesting, glee smug, knowing that no puppets would keep anyone from grasping their degree once they embarked onto that stage of life called next.

No such certificate awaited. I too (was and) had a grinning puppet, but in contrarian spirit was determined not to be one as I had done college wrong.

How? Mix equal parts anxiety and avoidance, late-night popcorn, coffee, and canvases, poetry, brain fog.

My father and mother never understood why I avoided marching to get my nonexistent degrees. The puppet had broken.

At certain ages, it becomes harder to get clear of puppetry. *To make a puppet look lifelike, first replicate breathing pattern, gaze, and stance*—first line of the literature-as-puppetry manual I began writing as senior project and then abandoned.

Because whose puppet did I most want to be? How to save your own life: a manual this probably might not become. How could I break free?

Long before, I had lost all chance of really learning whatever I could at that fancy school for which I had gotten a scholarship. Telephone wires twisted in the storm: the signified swallowed all, my hunger endless as anyone's, even the mean film producers in Los Angeles who nibbled from plates of cheese and olives at that outdoor restaurant where I would soon lose my first job.

One benefit of an undegree from that fancy college: when I returned west to the family, as if a farmboy gone east and returned, no dirt under the nails, just fine accents and collars, (mother's) sienna-burnt eyes glowed: what is it to become a person of interest?

The name of my college alone! Signifying I might know a thing or three about books and writing, her new and atavistic obsessions.

She—like what Roland says of his, the one he mourned—had in her own way *made herself transparent so that I could write.* Serving needs in the one case, absent in the other. *What have I to lose now that I've lost my Reason for living—the Reason to fear for someone's life,* says Roland, a few days into his mourning, the entry of April 2, 1978. All parents have ambitions: *the single greatest influence on a child are the unlived dreams of the parent* (says Jung).

In taking these notes (continues Roland, bereft) *I'm trusting myself to the banality that is in me.* Never be left and work hard; these sole mottos I trusted, banal yet what others can you believe?

Connivance

Both my parents could never be sick—they attended just about any outside pomp: the school concert or city spelling bee, liking the gilt others might slap upon my name. Certain people get this destiny: to live from *doing not being*, our culture rewarding the trait until the person can no longer do.

You're such a three (Uncle Rick, quoting the enneagram, would often say to me).

Reader, I also confess: long after my parents' hearth lacked a single ember, I find myself returned to their tribe: the ergomaniac, hoping not to spread disease to daughters.

While therefore I found it no miracle that my father showed up at graduation, I found it amazing that two parents could even stand breathing the same air, exchanging molecules and talking amiably—so long divorced, they no longer even lived together.

Part of their rapprochement or détente may have been due to the civilizing presence of Uncle Rick, north by northwest, mother's black-sheep friend, an odd bohemian character who gargled as if post-tracheotomy, wearing trademark fedora and long black leather overcoat, belted, his chestnut mustache curled as if unduly influenced in formative years by the image of Salvador Dalí.

In best get-up, Uncle Rick had sacrificed the cool opera ambience of North Beach cafés to smile blindingly fake teeth on a day made of gray eastern humid May. He forgave my father all crimes of absentee trespass, clearly, yet how hard for me still to forgive him all his incursions on me.

Some eleven years earlier, my father had gotten divorced from my mother, or she from him—stories differ—partly to save his financial skin, a bankruptcy of marriage and soul.

Yet on our father went living at home, only moving downstairs to the basement apartment. A family trait, this habit of being *messy with time* (my father hocking past for the future). Because of such miscreancy, we had detectives snooping around our home just to poke holes in their circumstance.

Did signifier fit signified? (As Vegas mate used to say about communication's own crapshoot, *you with me here?*)

Undo a marriage, you unfasten the signs like a wily coyote hellbent on making sure everyone stays confused: until death do *us* part? Until death does *its* part?

For months, mother and father could not emerge in public together. Skull and bones descended. Into that vacuum, our mother invited her brotherly friend to live upstairs. Between jobs, in permed-hair used-car salesman apparition, mustache copying one era's screenstars, Uncle Rick made a joke of blowing out all the candles on my seventh-birthday cake.

That cake still makes me sick, now and forevermore. Carrot with frosting, neon candy studding rim, but Uncle Rick had been the adult who remembered to wangle something birthdaylike, a little over-attentive.

My mother hovered, eyes lit from below, pleased at how quickly our unfunny unblood uncle made himself useful tending to kids, their needs and squalor. At his side stood my father, risen from the sepulcher, a person hanging from his shoulders. He wished me happy returns before sinking back to the lower depths.

When I retreated to my room to cry—is it any surprise?—it was Uncle Rick who comforted me. And more besides, starting the pattern.

My mother was at work, my brother with friends, my father in the grotto, or traveling to do good somewhere, and I had the luck of a house companion.

Important to make promises to your future you will keep (said Rick, witlessly setting the pace as we strode to College Avenue and its old-style stationery store). *Use this planner*—selecting slimline morocco for me. *See how good it feels to keep promises. To yourself,* he added (as if I could not see).

When, years later, I visited him in prison, in Marion, Illinois, I did not bring up the planner and all its promises. Because by then, Rick was on another kick: stealing vitamins on lunch rounds, *I'm light-fingering healthy years the feds want to steal from me.* (Hocking present for future due to past.)

Through a grille, he fed a mafia boss burgers, having gotten to be server for good behavior.

As ever, I lacked words to say; his monologue filled the therapist-prepared speech I had wished to shunt his way. If Rick stole years from me, that ends up not the full point of this story (though it may be a baseline). The point: mother is dead and without confession, Rick has become executor number two. Who knew mother would have appointed, along with sassy dancing shaman, this former tyrant to dispense worldly possessions to her children and granddaughters?

The idea of my parents' bankruptcy-cum-divorce? That, after a decent time, my parents—like those multiply marrying celebrities off Elizabeth Taylor Road—would reunite. That theirs was a divorce *in name only.* That they would rewed: one of those recommitment ceremonies of California, puffs of sage, everyone wreathed in flowers and hugs of deep feeling.

Both so wed to work, they never saw that recommitment day, furthering themselves in separate cultural seas, their parties boisterous and celebrated, filled with animated ottomans of octopi reaching out for hugs and my parents sailing by, happy schooners. They made a gift: a whole community of people who saw one another only amid their spray, Uncle Rick forever lurking nearby.

Occasionally my mother would bellydance and invite my father up to move his hips with her, loose, like a sheikh, and her Sunday-morn students would ululate, hands covering flicking tongues, all of us peeking into a performance of supernal passion, my parents smiling, their hearts seeming something grand, my father the abstracted scientist and my mother a carnal brilliant polymath.

Having met teaching folkloric dance, they carried this element of courtship forward but what hidden part of love deepened and what became pure operatic display?

And how did this message translate to my young mind? To be authentic, better not join forces with anyone? Desire leads you to the edge of the known universe (and then withers)?

Her death has changed me, I no longer desire what I used to desire (says Roland to his mourning). How can life redeem love?

Behavior

At the faux college graduation, as in the divorce, the two parents did not understand why I wished to walk apart from everyone, while Uncle Rick ended up with great urgencies every half hour involving bathrooms—his needs kept derailing others. Because Rick had a talent for making most events about (the great globe circling) him.

Accordingly, his biology overcame us, the rite become a map of his intrusive body, a detailing of available release, undoing plans for meals with friends and their parents—but why whine? Change was fortuitous: no one would press me about plans.

With relief, everyone from each cardinal direction retreated to our usual quarters.

Before that moment, quite high on early-adult alienation, I didn't wish to walk with either parent. I wasn't picking sides: I lived in pure lizard-brain survival.

My tongue knotted; the effect of fancy college hadn't shown up yet. So when they asked what I had studied, I could not explain how I had fallen amoureuse with one special figure from my school of specialness, one alienated figure twirling these themes: the progenitor of Os, Roland.

Have you ever known someone endlessly charismatic whose core you never quite reach? Impossible: Roland's words, their shocking contemporaneity.

Anyone who wishes can land upon this trick of the entitled, to wit: draw out your professors with dire incompletes, promises of summer work, apologetic emails. The white-glove establishment understands noblesse oblige. Many imploring notes later, make up credits in night school, and, if you wish, enter graduate school, and still you will get to start your career as a dedicated freelancer.

Only make promises you both care about and fear enough to keep (said Rick). And so on Roland, I have rested my entire career.

Why? Passionate and forgetful systematizer, impatient and whimsical, an improviser. Ravenous, revelatory, hidden, angry, refined, ready to theorize away feeling, leading whatever parade I wished to follow, his words behaved as I wished to be. Quiz for the alert reader: have you not wished to divorce body from mind, that particularly western paradigm? And follow someone who has navigated the distance with some elegance?

On this island, my longtime friend, a torn copy of my favorite Roland work, leans against the windowsill, against the utter consuming dark of this moment before dawn overtakes the slap of waves on rock. Could you be misled into thinking stray moments of exalted existence might stitch up something resembling coherent life?

To understand

What do you say of
someone who reads
a life and then thinks she
must go live it?

One fine melancholic acquaintance in grad school helped me move into a new room, carrying my few belongings, and, once we rested, revealed herself as a literalist. I will never forget what she said (was the name Kate?—her short sparse lank brown hair, pale heart face, friendly brown moon eyes shifting under horn-rimmed glasses, seen before me still):

I made a mistake (said Kate) *reading Henry Miller too young. He writes that girls with wide hips become whores, and so I followed that career path for way too long.*

(The signified leads the sign.)

Some people have found such literal paths. Not becoming authors but instead following destinies prescribed by their heroes' shadow imaginations: Achebe, Baldwin, Bukowski, Darwish, Faulkner, Kingston, Lee, Malcolm, Morrison, Narayan, Paley, Plath, Rilke, Rimbaud, Rumi, Rupenian, Salinger, Shōnagon, Tanizaki, Winterson, anyone.

Is it questionable that given the winds of my time I found it in Roland?

So restless (like my parents). Repudiated the old, and then, once established in the avant-garde, he went on to create a forward-looking science of literature so as to extol old heroes. (Hocking future for past.)

That enterprise he also abandoned. Carried an outsider's contradictions: successful, he didn't like meeting new people, so stayed in comfortable boîtes, the habits and cafés of Parisian environs. His truest shadows: also feeling himself to be blue trash, fallen from rightful inheritance, an overlooked kingly son contending with poverty, bouts of illness, the camaraderie of a sanatorium (health in drag, with its masqued habits an alt-academe).

From its vantage, he filled the coin-shaped hole in his psyche: envy toward the great and lesser gods of higher ed, Marxism his whetstone.

To have a chip on the shoulder: this a phrase I learned from Vegas mate: this badge of resentment, the chip for Roland a flaneur-warrior's epaulet.

Reading is a form of writing, writing a form of reading, understanding a form of cruising, dare to follow me if you will, I am on the sidelines of the expected, I will pop out and you will understand me if you dare. This (essentially) Roland crooned. How can an adolescent (and later) not love the song?

Sontag says: he is the one French theorist we will remember from the war. (Or the one we will recall from theory.) *Suffering lets you find the best,* he vamped, as if Christian or Buddhist. The clean air of the sanatorium let him avoid the occupation. Imagine you had youthful and repeated tuberculosis and a mother who worked so hard, cut from her vain salon-keeping mother's wealth: imagine you felt triply sidelined.

Natural that Roland would end up extolled yet not at the center, creating a haut-bourgeois existence with streets, delicacies, furtive pleasures.

My first encounter with the figure of the European intellectual: a high-school history teacher, Helmut in Berkeley's balmy Mediterranean airs. A cherubic balding older German man, stray ear hairs seeking higher frequency, who favored a certain café for a pastry stratified as an imperial court, some Prussian cloud-fluff and cream. Helmut wrote his own book detailing the entirety of European history as he saw it, personal historiography trawled all the way through the glorious German empire, spittingly articulated: the defenestration of Prague toward the abominable ahistorical consciousness of the Americas in which Helmut found himself.

Each day, a student was to repeat back the prior day's lecture (the past hawklike over us, circling). *Can we have a summary?* he would say, cued (as we all are) by habit. Is it useful to add that Helmut had been a fervent pink-cheeked flag-waving Hitler Youth? What could he make of his latterday incarnation as teacher to a flock of Californian students so motley?

His order suggested that history could be assembled in a compendium, a pharmacopeia in which remembered poison becomes antidote.

So when I call upon Roland, my mind sometimes conjures Helmut, at yet another café after another pleasant debrief with a comrade, surprisingly careless in brushing crumbs from rounded lips onto spattered lapels, crushing an ant on the table, and in California style, he rises, casting smiles all around the café as if otherwise the court of public approval could find something in his past amiss and eject him from paradise.

If you destroy one
life, you can find
yourself seeking its chains:
hypervigilance, walking
on eggshells, worry, fear,
flight, fawn. Without
your shackles,
unmoored.

Is new love heavy enough?
Can you attach without oppression?

Embarrassment

To sign your name to anything! How do you dare? The most humiliating requirement of early childhood, launched into a new second-grade class, the kids older: the signing of a clipboard hung outside the bathroom door. Much better to avoid such disgrace. Who wanted to author their body?

After some early incursions by Uncle Rick: never! Never author, never sign. Stay hidden.

Hello, said the future friend, *sorry, there's a puddle under your seat.* Imagine you stand outside as janitor is summoned, that you might then haul (avoiding shame from mother) a sodden garment back and forth in backpack until carefully shoving it into the back of a drawer (hiding from thwarting) your mother had carefully labeled MISCELLANEOUS.

The body and its miscellany. The enigma code becomes: tell no one anything related to your body. Instead, hide in culture. What part of the natural must you repress in order to live inside human culture? What section of the alphabet must be excluded? What words does your superego let emerge?

Body

You don't have to be a lizard
with that secret capacity for a new tail
to have some aspect of your life hushed.

That paradise of high school
was not immune: a different teacher
who, like Roland, still lived with mother.
An overgrown boy in long shorts biking,
leading scouts. Whispers accrued.
Or the black-bearded funny leader
of snapping eyes who brought a team
to the nationals until something led him amiss
in a hotel corridor, witnesses stacked
like Salem creamers, hysterically innocuous
in the lobby near the hospitality station.

There also sparked some kind
of touch in the zone
between the rumpled defiant chin of one sports coach
and the pert endless ballerina
impetuous competence
of another. The erotics of knowledge,
the flinty-eyed hope:
who wishes not to be understood?

Roland, known for positioning desire so clearly, did not come clean with friends. An era of closet and cusp meant he hid lust and hurt in text. Called a phenomenologist, he pressed all mushroom tendrils of hiding and observation into ink.

An orientalist about his own body, his extremities distended and foreign, he took such pleasure exiting it, since how much easier to believe you see the system once out of it. The book he most loved writing concerned the subject he knew least: Japan. As if the most pleasurable travel arose when wrapped in an unknown vocabulary, living inside the preverbal with one's own skewed consciousness.

A few books I read as an adolescent seem to have had disproportionate influence: Grace Paley's *The Little Disturbances of Man*, one I'd prefer to leave a mystery, and then the work of Roland.

About that Paley book: only last week did I realize that for years I had chosen as Vegas mate someone foreign to me but identical to Paley's wise-cracking men.

In this way, but not just in this way, marriage can be revealed as a recherché fiction. You keep believing the premise so you might continue the promise of rejuvenation. X and I told the story of our courtship out of the corners of our mouths; this, according to marriage scientist Gottman, is a dead giveaway. Soldiers of the apocalypse stalked our conversation: stonewalling and critique equipped our armory. Poor daughters, exposed to endogenous cortisol, their nervous systems left on high alert. One reason for the union's end this wish: to model for them a better fit: my heart's cry, not just post-factum mythology. I didn't want them to choose an angry mate just because certain modes—worried, tearful, or raging, far from any valorous, moderate Dorian—stayed our most common music.

From this fiction made too real, the father of three daughters, I diverted my path, and only now realize how much he spoke like some first book loves:

You don't look half bad, you know (says one of the men of Paley). *Don't laugh, you ignorant girl. I bought real butter for the holiday and it's rancid.*

Before I met Vegas mate, working as a butterfingered waitress, not yet knowing what undergirded my romantic life, I found three lines of Roland spoke to my soul, such as it was:

I am interested in language because it wounds or seduces me.

AND

Language is a skin: I rub myself against the other.

AND

You see the first thing we love is a scene.

A scene then: imagine you find yourself walking, after your undegree, the long hazardtape stripe of beach in Los Angeles near where you once traveled with mother to Muscle Beach, but you are thinking of Roland and his love of looking at cultural products as a series of myths extolling power structures of capital or desire, and random men shake themselves free from archetypal self-improvement routines to rake you with comments:

I'm an idea person, how about you?
Or: *how's your workout shaping up?*

Among other jobs of that time, I had a small radio show. Occasionally, I interviewed commentators, interrogators. A means of flipping the vector. To rub myself against the other of Los Angeles. Everyone there had invented everyone else. Everyone was an idea person. Each day asked you to contact the loving gaze of your own self-appointed church, a babe lost in the American wilderness of self-improvement, and the populace let you know your coordinates on their map.

Whom again did I interview? The short inventor of liposuction with his handlebar mustache plus his fast-talking genius girlfriend, allegedly his favorite work-in-progress with her well-contoured cheeks and lips of rubber (neé Celtic, most resembling an anime doll). She professed herself a *lover of form*. Also: the speed-addled self-anointed body-fluid sprayer boy inventor of performance art. The genial billboard model who invented contemporary dog-walking. The blockhead heir to the Day-Glo legacy. See in the dark. *No one knew how before me.* Asking them to be on the show undid society's catcall. They stepped through the black-cloaked hall into the studio with touching displays of vanity, preening before the two-way mirror and so becoming even more archetypes in the most transient time in my life. (The signified become the sign.) You could not help be moved by the varieties of human vanity, my own included.

By making myself transparent, I was also vain. Everyone is raw at heart. They entered, I established audio levels, and their comments rose out of the vast bubbling fear we all keep well-guarded inside. To see in the dark? Infinite hope tickled the edge of tomorrow's cosmos.

Imagine you interviewed all these inventors, sidekicks and appurtenances, and then submitted this document of discourse on cassette tape to a producer and somehow this served as one of your most legit post-college jobs.

Between interviews, I played music I loved. No one made any profit. That these recordings served any part of the common good was as apparent to me as to the makers of American cheese. The work of the studio time ended up beamed out somewhere over Iowa cornfields by something called the American Radio Network. Maybe a lone cornhand heard some of my ridiculous questions, driving his truck after a hard day's labor, following the dashed yellow line that led nowhere. Maybe migrants working over a soiled amber factory floor heard the static between the self-regard of my interlocutors and my wish to get them to speak their bare truth, degree zero. It is hard to penetrate between a person and their own idea of themselves, the hazardous task of both hair stylists and writers.

But all the while, foolishly, I took a bet on Roland, headed north to a big public school with summer gingko trees spreading the foolish scent of bliss next to seminar rooms, late nights in the library with the broken, crumb-brushing intelligentsia, to study everything about him. Humans are odd in how we strain to make ourselves believe we matter. And all this took place on the west coast, California with its slippery coastal sandstone logic where no human ever counts too much.

Now amid the melted snows of the east, human-scaled dwellings, I find myself in this increasingly wobbly enterprise of a strongbox, aiming to create sanctuary for three girls which depends on avoiding carpet vipers while aiming for the completion of a book about a man who loved the incomplete: the sketchy scrap, soot pendent at day's end, a silhouette waiting in penumbra.

Literature is the question minus the answer, he says, before dying along with the world's optimism.

Born amid world war, a critic of colonialism yet his own grandfather an explorer of West Africa, seeking to map it, Roland born between the Fall of Nish and the Battle of Ctesiphon in the era of the French cavalry's greatest bloodshed and worst offenses, a writer who went on to change how and what we read.

Come across an original
and any critique you might
form twists, since all critique
springs from the way
your original taught you to think.

During my undegree, I took those three classes on Shakespeare but found anything I would want to say about such shimmer to have been said already. Roland may have half-ruled some professors, yet no matter their insight, before anyone even shows up to read, already the Shakespeare play anticipates you. Any potential interpretation already embeds in the text, tiny little mirrors as if sewn onto a Moroccan purse. In such a mirror, you cannot see yourself, of course: the tailor has already anticipated your love of shine. This is partly why great narcissism must die in most text. You write something to surrender outcome: people often understand you as you least wish.

And yet if this investigation I am bound to write is not submitted, my new and groundbreaking inquiry into Roland, such as it has been touted to be—*Riveting! Promising to change the very nature of our understanding of inquiry! Engrossing! Bold! Bald! Brave! Revolutionary!*—our parsonage with its band of help meant to let us all thrive, like a peat disk made of manure which you impatiently loosen into water so that a store-bought dahlia bulb might find best sustenance—this entire flimflam structure will sink deeper than buried Roland.

How do you turn to a child and tell her you have failed? And in this most basic respect: keeping a house over everyone's head. Keeping it safe. If we were being shelled by mortar, I would be doing no better than I am with all this elaborate planning.

Perhaps it's useful here to recall that even hell has its angels. Also its hills and declivities; the very nature of hell is that it is not undifferentiated, there are shades, chimeras, near-misses, tantalizing strategies, escape, hope.

Quick interlude

Anyone might be forgiven for imagining some eschatology of future release. So easy to miss the greatest memo: contentment in the present. Until you get bit by the unexpected and learn what you must.

Which meant for me that in planning a major event (hocking present for the future)

I
ignored
the little bug
which bit my cranium in
its most ancient part.

One tick
bearing all the worst news
of evolution (that inexorable
juggernaut, pushing forward).

It was a time of augury: the end of spring when the outside enters your inside. Imagine that you turn to nature for succor, so it might mother better mood, because new habits revive when you overturn old earth.

At the start of summer, the tick you will name Midas bites you. Because you are tending others, getting a child or two toward a coming-of-age event, a job, a camp, helping others toward freedom or autonomy, you will not monitor signs that might spell your own dependence.

The innocuous act of pulling weeds up—how in life do we ever know what to call a weed?—does not help. You wished to put frustration elsewhere and the weeds returned the gift. A vast poison ivy rash considered first wrists and ankles ample terrain but then wished to plunder your whole being, making your face its own garden, a rise and spread until your eyes almost swelled shut. You could barely see out. Let us imagine your doctor will not recognize the rash, instead offering a scrip for a steroid you have never taken.

Should you stay alert to odd signs? The thing is never what it seems. At the pharmacy, the one who dispenses pills for the family, she lives in something like your own costume.

Platinum hair, penciled-in features, warm sienna makeup, late twenties. Hard to tell what she looked like at six but she probably would have been your friend in any embarrassing long-ago classroom, and you can see her a warm woman at eighty-two. You are also in a drag: receiving the medicine. For some reason you both quickly escalate into dialect, one probably known to teen girls on the Jersey shore, slathering each other with tender precepts about all the ways to manage life within a body.

> You'll be so fine, you'll see.
> Totally (you say).
> Just don't take it with milk!

Motheringly. And just as Winnicott's good-enough mother does for her child, the platinum pharmacist sings the future in which you belong to a genus of people who are well, where your health makes sense in a realm to which you belong, and how wonderful that there is some kind of consummation in meeting another person in dialect and drag, using that exact mode—the kindness of strangers—that has so beautifully mothered you so many years.

What happens when one is touched by a small poison part of a larger poison? Each of us swallowed by patterns larger than our control, all of us parts of the larger bacterium, and how can we learn what we need to learn from, say, the multiple intelligences in slime mold?

John Henryism, one daughter reads to me, *this*
is you! A strategy for coping
with prolonged exposure to stress such as
social discrimination by expending
high levels of effort—you can always work harder—
which results in accumulating
physiological costs.

The illusion that you can work harder as a means of controlling your circumstances can make a person implode, especially deleterious when you have a difficult roof of any sort—real, socioeconomic, emotive, imagined—over your head.

Have you planned for the great lessons of your life? From your current vantage, you never imagine your biggest lesson. Break bonds of the past, you might be forgiven for thinking you stand on a new plane and then also get to leave your mind back in baggage claim. Hold too many roles and you might stay clumsy playing the present: ex-mate, life manager, parent, other.

Do I stutter here?

Dependency

There had been mornings after her death in which waking alone into the morning made the vortical nature of my mind wish to drag me down, I could not find joy, and everywhere I looked lived the story of Atisha's cook.

The sage Atisha had a cranky cook and all the rest of his retinue asked: *please, tell us, Atisha, why do you keep him?* And of course Atisha said: *because that cook is my best teacher.*

After years of a relation the opposite of nurturing, in which I felt I needed to jump, walk on fire and then eggshells around the moods and organizational style of an angered mate, perhaps my brain got addicted to the neural pathway of negativity.

So what pleasure to wake one morning in the parsonage and find myself so happy to hear the music of the new love, who again performed with an ensemble last night in Los Angeles. To feel, for this second, I had arrived somewhere. Even in my messy room.

Remembrance

The pain of going through belongings after someone dies is that we all touch billions of objects in our one life. An old dramatist text on types of plot would organize such moments this way:

> It will be seen that the appearance of these figures of the second plan, these Choruses, Confidants, Crowds, Clowns, even Figurants re-enforced by those of the original groundwork, precursors whose importance ranges from Tiresias to the Messenger of 'Oedipus the King', from prophet to porter, modifies most powerfully the effect of the ensemble, especially if we reflect that each of these, considered separately, has his own especial motives for action, motives soon apparent in regard to the characters who surround him in some dramatic situation subordinate to the dominant one, but none the less real; the turns and changes of the general action will affect him in some particular way, and the consequences, to him, of each vicissitude, of each effort, of each act and denouement, contribute to the spectator's final impression. If the Third Actor, for instance, be a Disputed Object, it becomes necessary to take into account his first and his last possessor, the diverse relations which he has successively had with them, and his own preferences.

And so I stayed silent on the call with the beneficiaries.

> If he appear as Inspirer or Instigator, we must consider (aside from his degree of consciousness or unconsciousness, of frankness or dissimulation, and of Will proper) the perseverance which he brings to his undertaking; if he be unconscious, the discovery which he may make of his own unconsciousness.

What does it mean when you cannot understand the social awkwardness or fuzzy thinking of someone related to you?

> If he be a deceiver, the discoveries which others may
> make of his dissimulation ('others' here meaning
> perhaps a single character, perhaps the spectator) —

It is not my job to reveal
deception. The middle path
is to take

a walk near old grounds. Near the interregnum apartment where I possessed nothing, in which daughters and I danced at night in a living room bare but for its high ceilings, wooden floor, a futon from the street, a hammock that best friend sent. To walk by that place where I fancied myself a mother dedicated to her math geniuses. Every night, after homework, I rolled out a bed on the living-room floor by the heater for daughter #1, while #2 and #3 shared the second bedroom. We invited someone over for dinner; bowls of spaghetti were passed over my head while I sat on the stepstool and we laughed. We had no real table in the kitchen. To walk by that place was to walk by the world where

I had nothing, no membrane, no appurtenances,
a pupa flung out into
the world raw and sensate, as if
we could all be given chance
to begin again. A colored
bit of translucency
afloat. Seen through,
untied.

To touch what it meant to have a self that first year after the great sundering. Not as someone sheltered. But now we were shoring up foundation: even more terror.

What story could help us
find a way?

Fulfillment

Up the hill from the writing shed
where I have started work on this
Roland book tilts the grandly altered
schoolbus, camouflaged brown,
of the ecotenant who
moved in as if to make
(what seems now)
the hubris of home purchase possible.

The tenant would make the dream
of safety tenable. We would
exchange labor (his)
for his chance to bring
his *tiny home*, species *giant schoolbus* converted inside,
onto the land (ostensibly,
temporarily, only in legal terms, ours).

Such is the contract struck
by the communalism
of my childhood west coast:
I hoped for help and/or company.

Get what you wish for
but not in the form you choose:
perhaps I spent most daylight
hours of our ripcord
winter outside, shivering, talking
with the ecotenant about his
plans. My private hunch
is that he must rank among our
contemporary world's most notable
planners. A scientist-in-training,
a beanpole at that crisis
inflection point of twenty-five, a young man of

species *grad student americanus,*
of Midwestern vintage, so kind
in actual bearing, one might overlook how great
a proportion of his head
more than tickles clouds.

A Luftmensch: what a delicious word—an 'air -person'
or Atisha's cook in hiding.

The ecotenant's parents came
from Kansas and helped him
drill, tilting his home from seventeen
to twelve degrees. *Good for my core,* he says,
about living in a skewed bus
in woods abutting our
would-be simple home.

Any agreement we make, Luft always jots
carefully into one of two black
books he always carries
and then proceeds promptly
to forget. We have spent
so much time talking and
planning. Now and then, I see
him moving things
north to south: three stones, a rusted rake,
a branch, an extensible
shovel for snowy eaves. He moves
things and in this lies
his work; is writing any different?

I admit something
in the certainty of Luft's
movement pleases me
(a morocco slimline planner

toward future order).
My present leans toward the future.
You could imagine him with more
of a grip on reality, a more organized
sock drawer, when really he lives
in a bus packed with dishes
in untethered milk crates, its level twelve
degrees off plumb.
Yet how easy it has
become for me to
appreciate order in
everyone else.

Errantry

When you become a parent, much of your energy becomes a libido toward structure: how do you create parameters?

Here's the amazing aspect: Luft, not a parent, lives without order. His apologies are fine as midwestern cider, frequent, profuse, also with a touch of passive intergalactic force prone to electroresistive mishap: alarms are not set, time management falters.

Luft presented me with a boxed set of hand-pirated DVDs for a player I don't own for a movie about the cosmos: a gift to honor the solstice. He celebrates holidays with pagan precision. Always magneticisms zoom in beyond his control. To his breed of plaint, I am deeply sympathetic, as if we are all creatures fallen onto the planet by odd gravitational hunger, held under the moon in our spinning galaxy.

Perhaps this trait—over-sympathy, the heart that bleeds itself out until left for squirrels to nudge in their search among tall oaks for disappointed acorns—has led to our current state.

I call the discourse of power any discourse that engenders blame, hence guilt, in its recipient, says Roland.

What after all were Luft and I discussing all summer and winter? While I was supposed to be writing on Roland?

Where to situate oneself. How best to live. In other words: the best position for Luft's bus and my shed in which to write the opus for which I had hocked the family fortune (future for past) piddling as it is.

While discussing positioning, I was led off course and now must pay. The bills have been piling up in a giant hand-woven basket, as if a peasant's harvest. So repetitive, these creditors; they cannot help but repeat themselves. For both writers and bill collectors, lean syntax can become a pipe dream.

The basket harvesting all the creditors' bills teeters in a small former parson's room, a neat space with a fold-out desk, where the man once doled out his form of indulgence for those who had sinned.

At the bank, my main creditor, the mortgage official, is a swift numbers whiz with an algorithm of starched hair, smile, pearls, and perfume, all a deadly feint away from next month's risk: my foreclosure.

The bank itself—you too could be deceived—happens to be a cooperative seemingly run by a young pregnant woman soon on leave who sends me lovingly misspelled messages, her personal semiology: *sorry, your overdrown again :)* <:.

The last contract I had—one which put miso in the pot and bread in the frying pan, kids' favorite working-mother meal these days—was to write for an embassy an investigation into certain hushed-up killing fields.

Such contract work seems to have dribbled the last of a particular sum into my bank's account. Now the piper has come to be paid, the book on Roland overdue, and Luft our ecotenant moves branches east and south and then returns to his huge tilt of a bus where he occasionally sleeps under blankets though mostly in his lab on campus.

Reader, I got distracted. And now my survival brain has taken over: in writing this book, is someone riveting me? Actively shelling my shed. I stood there, worried about being riveted, the children soon to return back for their time at their father's house, and I soon fleeing with new love for this hospitable artist retreat of an island off Maine's bold coast.

A trend in dramatic irony which Barthes may have appreciated: the exact steps a character takes toward her greatest wish brings her farther from it. Where is the safe home for my children? (Me, gone. O, prayer: may I not be my absentee mother.)

Faults

Parenthood can mean the following: learn what you have repressed. Learn all you wished never to possess. See the shadowed mirror. We seek to recuperate whatever we were not given. Of course, you hope you could be better, you do the best you can, you walk faultlines and hope not to get stranded on the wrong side when the earth quakes, and yet you are human, and orient inexorably toward your humanity; each morning you fall into it.

And so it is with every conversation the child has about a dog. She wants a dog and is strong as a classic rhetorician, so well does every argument orient toward an ultimate end: having a dog. The sky is blue and this quality links with a dog's love of a peaceful day. She sees Uncle Rick's dog padding around, seemingly neglected in the house of dead grandmother, and so a trip prior to ripcord involves caring for Rick's dog, she lights up in happiness, a blaze that could swallow grief. How capably she marshals arguments about ideal ages, anxiety, college, futures. *We could save it! We could just take care of it back east for a while.* Out in the cold, taking a dog for walks becomes a more difficult proposition.

Say it is your last day out west after your mother has died and you walk dogless yet with newish love and daughter in the hills over the San Andreas Fault above the grand vista and bowl of the bay at what appears to be a predetermined hour for the lone lanky older intellectual men of all nations, those who have long lived by the bay, to walk their neat non-shedding canines.

(For this second, let) the dogs represent the men's bodies.

A Frenchman, a Dane, a Japanese grandfather. They have merged their intellectual lives with the beauty of the place and they walk alone, for a moment having traded the mess of human encumbrance for the uncomplaining dog, the problem with their collective triumph being that each sighting makes your child, your beautiful product of the mess of human encumbrance, the one who has just lost the last grandparent, find greater ballast for her argument, the ongoing one, the mission to have a dog who can understand her wordlessly and soothe her worst fears. The center is barely holding, let alone the handholding of you and your beau which *hurts,* she says. You understand, you cease; her hoodie she yanks over her head.

> *Can you tell me when you can talk again,* you say (frequent mother plea).
> *Twenty minutes.*

You have long since stopped holding his hand. Instead a leash strings taut between you. As if a joke for her at which she will never laugh. Unwilling recall: the moment walking a mountain road with soon-to-be-X when he had held your hand and because he had been unkind the day before, when you had been caring for everyone yet were bleeding after a small medical event, you found yourself nauseated by the rare touch.

Final condemnation, already exiting the body of the marriage, your body stayed honest if faulty. Your daughters had cheered at the sight of you two handholding but you cleaved, unable to fake marriage's leash, fallen into that fault of authenticity which Rick used to accuse you of over-cherishing. *Authenticity is such a value for you,* he said, *me, I like politeness.* For the marriage, you traded authenticity, wanting to take yourself for a walk, to find the peace of resting near someone safe.

Magic

There is no innocent
speech (says Roland):
all is puppeted by system.

You know your innards
are always revealed by what
most disturbs?

For instance, there lives a breed of man born after counterculture but before/in/after millennials who finds himself cranky mainly because of gender coding—manboys confused by their generation. Feminine at heart (to be essentialist) who wish not to play aggressor, soft inside but cloaked by stern justice-seeking principle. Or vice versa: aggressive within an armament of softly righteous words. Say you cross them, you are lost: they cannot survive if they do not see themselves on the side of method and the right. This sort is dangerous. Cross them and you land squarely on the list of the bad, a target for passive revenge.

To these wounded manboys, fathered imperfectly by baseball-cap-backward bros of the last generation, small questions sound like criticism. Advice therefore: never question much. These boys like to be hailed discreetly as both papa and provider because it was thrust into them how impossible it would be for them to attain either status wholly, raised as they were by absentee or secretly old-timey masculinist dads.

Similarly, there lives a kind of woman who uses holistic precept to best justify a narcissism so omnivorous, there dragons be.

It may seem I am on a criticizer's roll. Both kinds of dragons have crossed my recent journey; do you have yours?

My Vegas husband to me was exotic; no breed recognizable in my childhood out west! Not bad at heart, just scarred by ancient history.

Imagine you are no stranger to this question of how to occupy where you actually *are*. So much more fun to focus on other people's problems and wishes: you get to save others or spectate. You get to vacate.

For years I have been that little girl, as if locked in a tall plexiglass column: see out, never ask for anything, serve others' needs, don't speak up, be a fast study, don't be a burden.

No surprise: I have had a hard time letting others approach—and here the surprise: all the dangers of my marriage kept me in such shelter of reproach, my own and X's, I got to stay safe (enough) from love's sublime.

Once, while a young art student, in a first iteration, I found myself having to leave the room: the young woman model was too sumptuous, hair bundled atop, eyes a knowing drowning violet. To see her was to see Marxism die, as Brodkey says, but while drawing her, I underwent the grip of synesthesia, all symphonies gathered, angles resisting the round, her gaze an index card with a message meant only for me. Between poses, a perfume, she gathered a tropical robe around her shoulders, belted her waist: it was all too much. In spectating, I could no longer locate the good, my gaze a spray that left me empty, lacking signature, tag, identity. Imagine yourself a lawless child bereft of anything but appreciation. You can savor a moment overwell and then wonder what message lives in your own discarded bottle.

Such optimism led me to this isle. An early-morning person, before we fled here, I had been trying to stay up to find who had been shooting our refuge.

Tenancy, dwelling. How do any of us finesse the art of safety? I still am not sure what to say to myself, to Luft the ecotenant, nor to Biff, the subterranean grad student from the Alamo who only recently left our east-coast new home's basement room, semi-finished. Rather precipitously, I had bought the house (hocking our future), and then daughters and I found ourselves needing to travel before an opportunity expired (beholden to the past's dream of the future).

Together with an old friend, we created a restorative-justice creative workshop on a foreign isle, in a war-torn coastal town, useful, meaningful, empty, pleasurable, backfiring. Long story, not to be put down here.

We returned to find that Biff had not only moved into his room but had taken over the new home and entire basement, lining up Alamo posters, covering the back door with a flag of his hometown heroes.

Picture Biff: a grand young seigneur with lips sugar-scrubbed and the gelled curls of a contemporary Fauntleroy, welcoming us back to our newish home.

At least the girls did not fear; each of the tenants drafted to support our new safe life lacked the cis-male heterosexist energies of the frat boys alight on the street below, hugging it up to spread viral patriotic drinking-song parodies. Somehow these elements had amassed on or near this parsonage land to help support, last year, our illusion of the safe life.

Bulletholes started to appear, however,
like the holes in reasoning
which led us here.

Call the local sheriff about the incursion? We cannot. All have grown ever more wary of the sheriff's office, given what we have recently learned. The local newspaper in our proto-agrarian village, which supports its own ecosystem of a thirty-thousand-person state university like a seasonal spawning ground for salmon, has in its log helpful remarks such as:

Nude man seen running the agricultural fields northwest of the university in nothing but new biking shoes. Sheriff located one shoe but was unable to track escapee.

Or:

Neighbor reports thump on porch and unknown driver. University police came to investigate what is a form of mail-order package delivery.

Not known for having mind and heart in the right place, our sheriff—instead we have formed a neighborhood citizen corps of vigilantes.

We all wish to be adult. One trick: secret one part of yourself away in a red velvet box and enter the fray, show up in the world of signs, and return later to tend the one hidden.

Informer

One can also hide in admiration. The leader in our zone is Vida, an elder sibling in a family of eight who runs the bio lab on campus, a stalwart mother, skater, scientist, competent fun-seeker from the south where clean-air peaks made her stronger than most, her hometown the place where people come to tug ropes and learn how to be rugged autonomous American citizens.

Vida enlisted her family to help move my writing self into a shed, her boys carrying boxes of journals on Roland which I cannot ever hope to revisit, the markings of years made trivial.

And so she too is alarmed, she too has a stake: who could be targeting your workspace?

Our local officers are not obviously swigging racists (too aware of being watched by lone lanky scholars) but boys from farmtowns who chose the academy, willing to wink away balcony fratboy hijinks with their own collegial half-envy, the fratboy students themselves come here as if solely to inhabit the sign and mythology of *college boy*, all getting their voices, hooting *bro!* at one in the morning, from central casting.

Frisbee, beer, party—ways to negotiate late adolescent vulnerability. My middle daughter, wearing shorts on her bike, they terrify; the sheriff looks off into the right middle distance.

About the bullets? Don't call the sheriff, our Vida keeps saying, a woman of such speedy acumen it can be harder to understand those who falter, our messy home, my newish love who defies gender norm, myself, my daughters.

Call this the theme: having extricated myself from hell, I find myself anew in the one most like heaven. Here amid the competents, scrabbling to make amends. Who among us has a truly organized sock drawer?

Those with whom I have found myself, our new neighbors. In the realm of a perfectionist, mine, to falter feels (in my inner ongoing trial) like indictment.

What does it take to let
go of perfection?
Could this habit of self-
exile (not) travel
to knock elsewhere?
Must it always be
my forever guest?

Drama

I tried mentioning more about the bulletholes to Vida, who, in one of the nearby labs seeks the secret of existence—she oversees the ecotenant's working group—but for all her authority has time, in organized sectors of afternoon, after son's tutoring, to practice with him, twenty-five-minute timed spurts of soccer, golf, badminton.

Don't call the sheriff, she repeats, as if a backwoods woman, *nothing but trouble. We'll find them,* as if her son's nets alone could catch any intruder. And so it has been that though there appears to be a threat on the land, our crisis has started to assume a gravity no greater or worse than any other.

Water seeps into the grotto in which Biff of sugar-scrubbed lips was recently seen capable of great multitasking: texting, eating ramen, killing it at videogames, talking to Alamo parents, watching football playoffs on his mammoth nailed-into-wall high-definition screen, managing to avoid paying rent for three months.

In addressing everyone's needs, I have lost the central thread. While talking about how to make all these tenants' lives work well enough—not good enough, I failed to work on Roland, the Institute for Roland Studies now is folding, and someone is taking shots at us.

No one is anything more than a temporary dweller on this land, here where children and I were to make a new break.

New Year's of the float, new love and I were heading out toward the risk of an Indian restaurant. The last message of the year came from Vegas mate: *I should take you to court, at least one kid hates living with that guy in your home. But I talked to lawyers and just now decided I would not.* Happy New Year!

In the last years of the marriage, it became clear: fighting became our sex.

Perhaps the New Year's message was his version of my mother's Valentine poem: perhaps he missed some part of me.

Not to mention that we fought differently: *Californian speech is fake!* he would yell. I understood, having seen from Uncle Rick and others how much psychologically astute speech bears its own buried violence.

As a bulwark against hurt, you can internalize your aggressor, swallow him whole so you forever hear his voice: that can be your hope of taming whatever assaults. Once you accomplish this feat, it longer matters if he is there: the aggressor abides, you are tarred and so fail to recognize yourself. *Reactive abuse.* I ended up in the last years of the marriage imagining myself so fully unlovable, like Klee's etching, *Hero with a Broken Wing*, unable to fly or help anyone, unable to recognize myself.

Scientists now ask this riddle and I ask you here: how much of the time do you need attunement with another to have a healthy relationship? What do you think?

Only thirty percent.

Thirty percent of all hours, waking or not, attuned with your beloved. That is all. If one-third of the time, you are dreaming, spooning, or present, aware of the other, your child, lover, friend, or reader, your gaze, heartbeat, and sympathy aligned, your loving attachment will do just fine. How are you doing? Not an innocuous question. Love requires tremendous heroism. Are you attuned? To go back to Klee: does at least one of your wings work?

SOFT

What I remember

Not historic dates but lines of dialogue between new love and me, the colors of shirts he wore but not capitals, not his full lineage with its names, but I will never forget how the angle of light slanted from behind his head on the streetcorner that day before we began when we shared poems by heart, whether he sat on the left or right as we faced the ocean, not the content of misunderstanding ever, that so quickly forgotten, my survival technique, perhaps you too share it, but that I wore his dark blue sweater, feeling myself a college girl as he bent his knees at that first goodbye hug in the train station.

Errantry

Every gathering at our university
has as its suggested preamble:
I'd like to begin
this event by acknowledging
we stand
on Nonotuck land. I'd also like
to acknowledge our neighboring
Indigenous nations:
the Nipmuc and the Wampanoag to the East,
the Mohegan and Pequot to the South,
the Mohican to the West,
and the Abenaki to the North.
We are temporary in all ways,
some less justifiably.

And now it seems—to turn the focus personal—this little family is about to become a little too pro tem. What happens next? The bank seizes control of land I've already desecrated? X gets to gloat? Children and I move to the homeless shelter, now conveniently located two doors down?

There is only one way left to escape the alienation of present-day society: to retreat ahead of it (says Roland). Life is endlessly ingenious in multiplying opportunities for loss. Consider the tree that had been sacrificed in order for the Luftbus to enter. In the end, a great oak with roots gnarled wide, favorite shade-tree and refuge of youngest daughter, had to be sacrificed for what we termed Luft's highway, which he called an alley, so that in case of the apocalypse, Luft our ecotenant could drive out, solar panels intact. Would you call this an example of sacrificing ends for the means?

What does Roland say about ritual sacrifice, a vertical means of understanding one's life, seeing one's sins go up in communal smoke?

From a course of lectures Roland gave at the Collège de France in the late seventies, on *The Neutral*:

Where there is
meaning, there is paradigm, and where
there is paradigm (opposition), there is
meaning . . . elliptically put: meaning rests
on conflict (the choice of one
term against another), and all conflict
is generative of meaning: to choose
one and refuse the other is always
a sacrifice made to meaning,
to produce meaning,
to offer it to
be consumed.

And what did we
lose as a culture when we
gave up ritual sacrifice?

I gave up, reader, and most days find myself looking at a heap of logs, stumps, behind which a huge tiny home looms.

Gradiva

Months into the float, college students convene. Fifteen of them press together furiously in a party room and spread glitter everywhere: numbers toll. In reaction, as Orwell might have painted it, outside the dormant giant of the ice-skating rink, squadrons of students line up, obedient, masked, gloomy. They present numbers, hold vials, follow arrows on the ground to where a nurse behind glass watches them twirl a swab in their noise, replace it in a vial, offer up numbers. They pace outside, tested twice weekly. No Gaia, no earth mother, could have imagined such a scenario. No goddess can tell us how we brought this to pass. No one feels mothered by our moment.

The gift you imagine giving the neighbor who acts as your friendly mother instructor, Vida, the one who seems to have her act together, is pumpkin pie, a simple human interaction with nature. A great umber dragon of dried leaves chases its tail at your doorstep. Thanks to travel and research into Roland, you had been able to take your daughters to see the world. In the new containment, you are glad that, even as the world shrinks to your driveway and these rampant colors of fall, you gave them the chance to see beyond your nation and town of scuttling fall leaves.

Vida shows up during this time in a multitude of ways. She organizes people for skating expeditions. Often she brings food in unbreakable dishes and offers to teach your children how to make spanakopita and other tricks in which you feel your lack of motherroot becomes obvious as an oak stump. Your car breaks down and she drives you to the auto shop, having skillfully popped out some multilayered pastry for her kids who are obediently helping set the table. On the drive, you marvel at her efficiency.

Next day, you go to the local vast market since you cannot keep up with your three children's appetites: you are on a treadmill, offering this meal and that, vanishing quickly into their maws or the compost. *You used to cook better,* one says. *Now we have snacks and fewer meals.* But when you put great thought and care into the meals, one or another doesn't like them, and the task becomes a highway of diminished reward (behind you, as you try working on this Roland book, one scrapes her plate). Perhaps the morning meal had been almost acceptable. Yet the glass measuring cup used to serve the puppy shattered; the puppy food must be thrown out in case glass shards cut up the dog's intestines. Instead, you serve the dog some of the pseudogourmet meal you had tried cooking for the kids, after the toilet flooded and the excavator came too early at the ecotenant's behest to lay the groundwork for another of his deferred dreams. Storm predicted for the weekend.

Your morning therefore had been crowded. Autumn falling, and so at the vast market you buy your neighbor both premade pumpkin pie and flowers you believe to be marigolds, with their connotation of domestic bliss and ease. In the afternoon you will give her both.

And yet you find a slice neatly cut by a child out of the gift. Not even meant to be a homemade gift; just a fresh offering. And instead all three of your daughters begin explaining, at once: one had peeked in, curious at the perfection. Crust shivered tectonically, pie imploded as a sinkhole, cardboard did not fit back into itself. Another, feral, tried to fix it by licking the center of the pie. The third then celebrated or assuaged the guilt of the other two by cutting an actual slice.

The gift to Vida who seems to have her act together: gone, licked, sliced. Such is the muscle you have been trying to build in your mind ever since the implosion of the marriage, you choose not to care. What a fabulous opportunity the world offers you: your boundaries are becoming swirled ink. Once, you were a world-traveler, no need to make borders; just move on. Here, firmly stationed, you must learn the trick: see through all walls, let it all dissolve.

Say you never learned during your time with X that a person gets to state boundaries. Instead, a nervous system might have become so dysregulated that you no longer heard the dancing skitter of leaves across a field in the fall.

Instead of the pie being
brought, it still sits in the fridge,
part of it licked by game-playing child,
a sign:
aspiration for belonging
plus the eternal incomplete.

Absence

My mother: she
was an incomplete novel.

She too invited in the surprise guest—the small element that starts to loom—a trait her granddaughters also have taken on, yet my mother, a dramatic scientist, did so in orderly fashion. Outtake, for example: the week prior to my father's death, I'd been pleading (such had become my role in the family) for her to consider hospice for him, in the nursing home where she had him stationed. Of course such choices are understandable and yet also predictive, somehow: she had tired of his having caregivers in her house waking her at night. She confided, furthermore, that she worried, in truth, about the mess—logistical? emotional?—of a body dying at home. Solution: his dying outsourced.

Though I spoke with his doctor who also thought hospice timely—titrating the meds that soften our end—this same doctor made the mistake of leaving a message on my mother's cell.

I then received a very upset email and voicemail, both, from her saying the following: *I have no time to deal with this question of hospice in the nursing home because I'm too busy preparing for my one-woman performance at the Moosh in San Francisco on the experience of living with a dying man.*

Imagine the Kafka story in which the artist keeps the dying subject alive to get content.

All that said: postmortem, I flew to see my father and his waxen head gazing up, a stone-faced Lincoln lacking comment on what he had just seen. In death, he stayed front row at a performance: outside the door, a stranger chanted ancient time-banishing ritual for him, the words life's substitute lexicon. The muttered prayers made clear the cliché that became so obvious I had to go live it: life is no dress rehearsal.

Once and never again, says Rilke in the Ninth Elegy, once and never more. You die having delivered yourself of all gifts (eggs, other) that were yours to offer this brief life. So why care about the particulars? We perpetuate details, acting as if ledgers matter, and we must learn again in detail the joys of a thin-veined leaf, the wonder of its spiral down, even if smashed by a bus, even if your shelter lets in winds you don't choose, this too has to be celebrated as part of the journey. So why is it so hard?

Her head

It also became incomplete, contested territory. Toward the end of her life, as mentioned, she had two thick horns atop it. Dying can turn the most flamboyant into their most feared monster.

That story of those last days:

Wilhelmina who works with her in the daytime puts oil (olive, coconut) on the horns, which Frieda, who works nighttimes, complains about.

I just want to clear my record, Wilhelmina tells me. *I'm not the one putting her hair in braids, don't listen to everyone.*

Two dreadlock horns: thick
thwarted heart shapes with the

narrow point starting a half-inch
from the head, a whorl of

origin matted in a tangle of
desire unmet. This the pain

of dying, the asymmetry of desire met
by the outside world. The hair dreams of

length, the imagination of flowing
chestnut locks, the hair testifies to

all. Instead the ends find
one another, swirl, the tangle

replicating what happens inside
to the ganglia of a mind

fed by cannabis and the untwisted noose
of poppy petals.

Morphine is the best: it doesn't knock her out anymore, she can still converse.

What a long dying does often—not always—is bring out the singularity of the person. In this case: mother's sweetness, a hopeful young girl forever ready for the party, lower teeth jutting forward as if thereby she could catch life, chew off some last twist. This the stilled underbite she used after someone complimented her, or at any bliss, the lower part of her face bunching with the joy of a squirrel, the smiling clenched kisser, eyes lustrous, loving shared pleasure. A face used when recognizing some silliness of both self and world but also when noting the world was there to savor. Teeth not especially straight or white. The relic of the childhood she did not have, the life which (thwarted) mother hoped might be hers, a mother whose thimblework helped with the quick patch-up job. Mother's tender older sister, honey running in her veins, stayed in the nation's heart and lived the dream of (thwarted) mother. Her *swimming pool was paid for by clipping coupons,* as caustic-tongued grandmother explained. Mother's sister lived the dream: offering an unthwartable gift of local clans, battalions of great-great-grandchildren. A vast world swarming with weekly metabolism: games, sports, meals. The glisten of pool outside, and inside, a pool table flanked by twinkling well-thumbed glass jars of jellybeans. Sister knitted and crocheted, received (unthwarted if conditional) love, created perfumed champions with straightened noses and white teeth with only the grandchildren divorcing. Families usually have only one black sheep. What my mother has in her dying: new wisdom.

She gazes distantly. I tell her, without going into the kind of detail she loves, the pith and tang she repeats back, some of the stories she has told me of her childhood. Only school offered her true love and horizon, a place to be recognized.

O yeah, she says, winsome and hopeful as if brushing up against a distant wraith of self, a figure flitting on the moors.

Toward death, you recognize the lineaments of rewards that have come your way.

And can elide the failings. What you have inferred and then come to know: poor mother had been caught touching herself and (in the grips of thwarting) her mother asked diligent father to hold the girl down so as to paint fire—mercurochrome—pouring it on groin and down her legs so that young mother's walk to and from school became a walk of shame. See mother as a young girl then: head held high, tall and straight in handsewn skirt with unwashable crimson streaked down the back of her knees above scrimped-for American bobbysocks and the penance: having to answer questions all day. Flee, don't desire: that could be the legacy.

This story my mother only told me upstate, long after I was the age she was when she had me. Angelic, she showed up after the birth of third daughter, sitting there rocking as I nursed. For once, needing to find out how the cord of maternity had been cut, the grisly, evil sentence, I queried.

And to mother's credit, umbilicus clipped, she still wished to spare kids her own suffering and rarely criticized, offering instead, as for many guests, the philanthropy of a house with her absent. The motherroot cut and so I had to pull out the story: who had done what to whom. What made early childhood hard. Bitterness of mercurochrome. At some point in her mirrored room, the room in which she will die, I arrange a bouquet before her, flowers passionate, crimson, redemptive.

O yeah, my mother says, as if bashful at their beauty, with the exact softness of a young girl.

Performance, war

Nights lubed and epoxied toward
dawn, a performance and war
take place in the same zone:

for no one but me, choreographed
by the oddities of human
quirk and history, in a privately

darkened room, a wild struggle.
This skirmish with victories and
war announcements takes place

between the bony calves
of mother and the angel
named Frieda with her gloved nighttime hands:
both are hard-working presences. On the side of the legs, testament
to mother's decades of work
as an Oakland civil servant,
insurance grants mother this last
gift, the chance to hire caregivers.

Frieda came through her own hard childhood and kept finding
herself going up the chain in corporations, in offices,
but instead prefers to be her own nighttime boss-angel
and work with the dying, she says,
I like to be useful and your mother's still
useful, she should still live.
Her hands slide up and
down with unguent drawn

from the teats of sheep.
The lord is my shepherd, I shall not want.
In that psalm of David, the sheep

find themselves splayed face-down in
the field, delighting in and
accepting their limitations.

Sunset Boulevard

Like a caul of grace, some great astounded humility has come over my mother. Perhaps she has accepted the basic sheepishness of humanity. We graze and savor, we move on, we pause in wonder.

And so she submits, grateful, to the warm ministrations of Frieda, who does good while narrating all that she does (no different than any writer, an echo). Is a deed good if it is not narrated? Maimonides says the second highest charity, among all strata, is generosity given anonymously; the highest rank occurs when you help someone to be self-sufficient and no longer in need of charity. Perhaps Frieda's narration has more to do with a quirk of her church and less with herself. *Your mother is finally so happy, she is dancing with her dead husband,* Frieda will sing at the wake, doing a cha-cha to demonstrate mother freed of earthly care.

But before all that, something drops into the world predawn, such a strange quantity, a pair in mortal combat. I wake at 3 AM and for my passerby hearing, Frieda strenuously rehearses what she is doing, vicious spasms of movement as she raises the leg, sets it down, her commentary thus: *Sugar, let's show your daughter here what we do here!* The skeleton legs obey, rotors of joints, my mother prone, staring up as if a wreath of crumpled flowers hang over her and she cannot have her attention veer off, a woman motionless but forever striving toward a goal. *Sugar, let's show what Frieda does with you EVERY MORNING!* The legs bend and straighten. The truth (as was often the case for me with my mother) is that I lack stamina for viewing (every) performance of love.

Around the dying, I have learned, you often find a certain kind of person gathered close, the moth-eaten hunger of someone hoping to be recognized. This being as true of me as any visitor. Because death is so asymmetrical, one needs to feel affirmed by at least one set of eyes, which are, depending on one's belief system: worldly, divine, neighborly, self-congratulatory.

I am visiting
the dying, I am helping
the dying, the dying
saw me.

Those of us born into motherlack may know it as a hole in the solar plexus, anaclitic depression, or achievement hunger, and so my mother huddled with me in belonging to the tribe of poorly mothered daughters. In a poverty-stricken immigrant ghetto, her own clever mother would have preferred to be a journalist, someone hard at work at a typewriter, using that caustic wit to incite revolt, but instead lost herself in sharp-tongued gossip at the canasta table.

This grandmother lost the universality of kindness along the way. She had four children, pitting kind eldest daughter against the other three: my mother the one who got farthest away, using mind as passport; another sweet sister, burnt by critique, lost a son, loved other children, tended frogs in her enamored palm and ate herself to death; a brother so favored he ended up in jail for cleverness, the one for whom the state of Mississippi changed its blackjack laws, and that friend of his, the wingman who became my unblood uncle Rick. Who among them counts as black sheep?

As my mother gets made up for the visit of the hospice man—the Baptist chaplain whom Frieda calls mother's boyfriend, with his earring in one ear, divorce and four kids part of his precociously world-weary baggage, who says that she, too, has become his friend—my mother's smile becomes that of the winsome haloed debutante her mother wished her to be, the one raised high in the photo by fraternity boys who voted her their black-ringleted jewess queen. Deep into a last myth that will keep her alive much longer, the monster of desire offering its final gift, my mother narrates the arrival of the hospice chaplain as her date coming to pick her up:

He likes to come see me, to talk of theater and friendship. He has other people and things to do but he likes to see me, it is practically as if every time he wants to have a party with me. And more: *we are having a party all the time together! He is always with me!*

I tell her, as in *Sunset Boulevard*, she is ready for her close-up. She misremembers the film, quotes another, her bird-boned hand creeping up her neck, and six months later it turns out she was mostly right.

His voice on the phone echoes as if through a tunnel: *I loved your mother. There are always certain patients whose being is much bigger than whatever life they have left. Doesn't matter the time you had with them* he chokes *you love them forever.*

Festivity

Why did birthdays so matter in our family? A chance to be called out from the collective. A chance to be seen for your birth alone. Some hearkening back to old-timey nostalgia. A chance to do it differently.

My mother's favorite game:

a string strung over everyone, mouths gaping at marshmallows strung at different heights. The mother jiggles the master string, mouths gape. This of her mothering habits you retained for your own kids' birthdays. Marshmallows and pretzels, the food going to the mouth of the most eager aspirant.

This game resembled her wake, the shiva: one almost didn't know she wasn't there. We gaped, we consorted, we felt her nearby: you can find comfort in such a game.

Gradiva

The hero of Gradiva *is an excessive lover; he hallucinates what others would merely evoke* (says Roland), and the object of this love, she, *she enters into it a little.*

She *consents to play the part of Gradiva, to sustain the illusion somewhat and not to waken the dreamer too abruptly, gradually to unite myth and reality, by means of which the amorous experience assumes something of the same function as an analytic cure.*

We try to play the role without precedent of script, the constructed family of new material; every other week three children and dog, chaos and laughter descend. (There are scripts for such schedules, the horrific new learning of divorce algebra premised on emotion, all of which we rejected: such as 4,4,7,2, as in four days on with kids, four days off, seven days on, two days off, every number marking the length of 24-hour periods with which those who came from my body can be with me. Week on, week off—did it not seem simpler? And ours was called a collaborative divorce, using only one lawyer, those sessions tense in a small lit room as we aimed for composure while I sought to recognize the generosity in which I had wished to believe all those years.)

Then Jonathan said to David, really, whatever
your soul desires, I will
especially do it
for you. So that David said
to Jonathan, look, how about tomorrow
the new moon when I cannot fail
to sit with the king
as he grinds away at his meat: but instead I will
go, I know how to hide
myself in the field
(and you might meet me)
(can I be met?)

Consider that in their new roles everyone must balance delicate teacups on thin trays on their heads; given the collective wish that new beau's be a featherweight presence during what also happens to be the time of our float. New beau holes up in front room with organ, accordion, and kitchenette where Luft first lived, love hiding so that no one feels too chafed. He is good at making himself a light presence, and affection for him flows, yet the strafing starts, my body become a battlebridge over which energies tramp. We have in our future a land of ease, yet sometimes it seems too much to hope for armistice or even détente; I cannot help my vigilance about how the daughters feel. The divorce came about in large part because in our old home, there was no refuge for me simply to get to be a mother with them.

We are all getting along, says new beau (skewing toward the positive and picturesque as late father did). *You are stressed by how everyone is getting along* (says eldest daughter, by contrast), *last year you were a jungle cat, you were better.* In her last year of high school, in our strangest moment, she is prone to metarecognition. *You and I, we do talk, we talk all the time.*

What do we talk about (I ask, as if predicting amnesia. The most recent science says that if neuroticism pairs with high conscientiousness, you can possibly bystep late-life decline even though no one gets out of here wholly unscathed).

In the kitchen you and I talk of my father (to my chagrin, the addiction rears its head), *in the dining room we talk of food.*

That's it?

You need to get back to caring for yourself (she says). *This year you are fire and air, you need more water. You need to start an orphanage in Portugal! You need to worry less about who is getting along with whom.* The friend says: *All your problems are with the earth element—how you create good structure for the family.*

It will be said to the lover (says Roland) *or to Freud: it was easy for the false Gradiva to enter somewhat into her lover's delirium, she loved him too.* Had I imagined too forcefully we could all live together peaceably?

Vouloir-saisir

In the middle
of a different tournament—
the argument—based
on early childhood
trauma, I learned it
worked to
go possum.
Play dead;
have Stockholm
syndrome, identify with
the captor.

As Roland says, considering
Dante's concept
of the Vita Nova,
a poetic and narrative form
to express love and mourning:
Two contradictory paths are possible:
Liberty, Hardness, Truth
(to reverse what I had been)
or
2) Laxness, Charity
(To stress what I had been)

To freeze, to go dead, to give
up, partially to reverse!
To not let *the soft animal of*

your body love what it
loves, as everyone
quotes the contemporary poet,
but instead to let the soft pink
fog of dissociation
roll down my front:
this had most often been

the unchosen pick
of long marriage,
the opposite of ultimatum.

To disown.
To sever body from head.
The unstated middle way
of the Vita Antiqua:
my old life.
Not liberty/hardness/truth
nor laxness/charity.
Just dissolve!
Free to anyone!

You could go foggy at front and let your back become a carapace, stiff as Kafka's own beetle or roach, however one translates *Ungeziefer*—monstrous vermin, an animal unfit for sacrifice, from the proto-Germanic *tibra*.

Offering, sacrifice, victim. You might let your body become these things. And afterward, call yourself survivor, not victim. Or, taking cues from the pink fog, call yourself nothing, since dissociation offers such ultimate pleasure: you feel nothing but the numbing of your nonchoice.

Was marriage Hobson's unchosen pick or Occam's razor? Did we think we were making the simplest choice for which our epigenetics equipped us? Was it Zeno's paradox, the arrow never quite reaching its mark? As if one day those arguments would achieve actual release. A happy ending, as a red-light masseuse might say?

I thought we would be like two cats in a bag punching it out, Vegas mate said somewhat disconsolately, also handing me a touching note of apology for talking badly about me all those years to everyone, in the corridor of divorce court where I had teared up after the female judge asked her most terrible final question (wait for it, a query required by law). Memory torques, that faulty corkscrew releasing venomous vapor.

Of course you can make any relationship *work*. But at what cost? Parts of my body had started to be cut off with scientific method. It seemed high time to leave parts in the trap—Roland's abandoned rib!—and for the sake of all (daughters, me, even Vegas mate-in-his-better-future) to move on. I didn't feel I had survived childhood to end up unfit to live for my kids.

You divorced so you could be happier, youngest daughter said, angry at the start, accusing me of the crime of being for my self. Running on a landscape from the cloud of selfishness. Hillel says: *if I am not for myself, who will be for me?* but also *if I am only for myself, who am I?*

After trauma, they say, travel forward. Establish gratitude practices. Say thank you to each morning and meanest flower, the universal wind, the tallest tree, stray leafshorn twig. Thank you, light, shadow, gnostic binaries, thank you conflict that lets me appreciate what I have now, syntagm, thank you for all that led me here, healthy, with children in this house, unusual boy tenants, these sheds.

Perhaps I did not mention there are two sheds. The other one, tiny, meant to be a mellow replica of the writing shed in which I write on Roland, a space for daughters and during our quarantine float, their friends seeking shelter. *There is only one way left to escape the alienation of present-day society: to retreat ahead of it.*

The tree stood amid sheds and bus and was sacrificed, much like the marriage the year prior. As if airdropped into a new story trying to make do, tugging the ripcord of this time, everyone making do, I've started to feel out of myself, more air and fire as daughter number one said. *Ungeziefer*. I hoped for a safe domesticity of the sort Kafka aimed to flee.

Plot twist: a scene: late night, the dog needs a walk. Youngest daughter and newish love take on the task most often. This time they head out and she speaks dispassionately: *the divorce broke me, we are in this new place, I will be in high school and one sister will leave, and I have only just a few years, I need my mother back—this time solo, maybe just a year!—with not you, New Person, I need mother to live with only me. Now.*

Now means do not worry about tomorrow's trouble, for you do not know what the day may bring. Tomorrow may come and you will be no more, and so you will have worried about a world that is not yours! Or at least so says a text sliding into our consciousness from 600 years before the common era. How easy, however, not to worry: as if that slide into the future connects your past with your present.

A story: say you once stood at a coming-of-age ceremony in which the religious officiant stuttered, as he did not know what to say to the young and potentially shallow adolescent who stood before him, someone who liked fashion magazines, primarily. What he ended up offering was great warmth, since everyone so loved the parents, pillars of the community. *You are,* he said to the young girl whose lips were glossed by the sexualized petroleum-product simulacrum of her hoped-for bubble-gum future of smackery, *you are a prophet of the now.*

The phrase could pucker the hearing. What is a prophet of the now? Someone who knows how to savor and love this moment? Can you become such a prophet even amid your troubles? How can anyone survive, let alone be happy?

In a place where no one behaves like a human being, you must strive to be human—so says one sage. Despise no one, and call nothing useless, for there is no one whose hour does not come, and nothing that does not have its place, says another. And our days are scrolls; write on them what you want to be remembered. These sayings wallpaper your cranium, layered in you marrow outward. How to become a prophet of the now? Among all we are trying to do and recall and avoid, is it not a wonder that any one of us in our time can still breathe?

Inexpressible love

Why is it that singing
of happiness veers so

quickly to banality?
I would never wish to live

near the seashore, said once
to me by an heiress, *too many*

other people seek that lifestyle.
Is a thing known by singularity?

I used to make an art of not
just holding myself away from

others, but prizing only what my
eye could see: not the screenstar

celebrated for dimples, but the short fast-talking
neurotic. My eye was (all that remained

of) me: if I curated, I was known.
Some may have nostalgia

for the old-style video or LP shop
with the bossy curatorial clerk:

what great societal role the clerk served, telling
clientele: you don't want *this* one, you

want that. (Instead, now we're served by
predictive aesthetic genome,

algorithms, synced pop songs of idiocy
that I learn from my teens, careening

around my head,
signifying?) Before and yet

still, we wanted to like something
few others did: as if this would confirm

the ruts and grooves
of our own trajectory.

The singular image then: a gentle
sleeping morning shape, the genderless

mountain of new love, atop morning
blankets, in bed, supple and plain,

bare to the elements.
Maybe you have finally learned

that a person's sexuality stands
apart from yourself in its abandon and

specificity, that it will not consume
you in its seemingly you-specific

fires, but has its own logic and trajectory,
and yet/so all the more suggests

itself as a gift. A person lies there with
abandon, ready, pliant, available.

you do not curate it; it exists
outside of all your eye believes

it is loved for seeing.

Ode to awareness

One thing remains apparent. Find a relationship ending and you may believe you have given more, giving and giving up. Do you have a right to grieve if you helped choose the end of the relationship? What is lost? Is it odd the addiction is still to the possibility of making it right for everyone, to be included in the familiar burr of his voice, as if you could be enfolded in the us-versus-them tribe he offered and get harmony back? All addiction continues because you believe you might get something good with the same bad habit still and yet again. You began with X when you were ill, you got better, and it all ended when what happened between you made you more ill, when you wished for the sun on all wounds.

When beginning with X, back in your early days of Manhattoes, you imagined every part of you could be healed if you had just three months with a love golem who could tend you as you had never been tended. There appeared, however, no fairytale love golem; you were never healed, you still felt bad at heart, and the relationship with X started on its uneven keel; once you found him when he had stormed out on the steps of a giant metropolitan institution and it seemed kismet as well as his rage asked you to stay together; is that even possible? How much of your life have you spent worrying about other people? Why does someone's twisted look bother you?

Let us say you were that child fearing everyone was angry with you—your survival in question—and then with your children you might feel as if you helped create a reverse love golem: a child who can always find reason to be mad at you.

That's yours, the genius friend counsels you to think, *yours, you can keep it until such time as you wish to bring it up.* How odd—you have always thought everything was not anyone else's but really yours to fix, that you were everyone else's love golem. Instead, can you be rooted like a tree and not give over to everyone's winds?

And do you have the right to grieve the percentage of time you have given over to worrying about others? What is grief? Can only the sun name its layers? (As I write this, a ladybug tumbles onto this page, spots uncountable, stopping to sniff the markings, the smearable ink of my pen, before choosing to fly away.)

Faults

Does memory serve?

By inviting ecotenant Luft in, I believed that as much as divorce had gotten us off the grid of conventional storyline, I would support the good life of a decent, kind individual who wanted to live out back, on land, off-grid in all ways, far from lines of convention.

The talk of which tree had to be sacrificed for schoolbus highway blurred in last fall's lopping cold. The two of us spent hours hearing all sorts of hard-boiled men wielding chainsaws, calling themselves *tree people*—as if a serial killer would call himself a *people person*—come and give estimates, the ecotenant and I sudden business partners, both of us oddly committed to his dream, a safe roof over his head. I wanted to keep my word as the marriage (sundered) had not.

Let Luft have his huge bus. Let the prayer of safety for everyone hold. Let people be people people, tree people be tree people.

Together on many moments the ecotenant and I stood, on our improbable hill, listening to these men, raw-faced and blistered, who eyed this skinny beanpole, Luft with his dark glasses, marzipan skin, and angular stance, his polite midwestern listening into which they spoke their own deferrals.

Yeah, they said, *you're a dreamer, sure, man, I wanted to do that once. I'd love to go live in the woods too!* (said with scorn for any modern-day Thoreau). The bitterness of the dream deferred!

They mostly told him how improbable it was he could have his future without vermin-laden varmints eating out the undercarriage of his bus.

Everyone sang mortality. *Boy, maggots will come!* each said. Each in turn found new and exciting ways to try to tell him his dream was one big fat bad idea of loss.

We invited their expertise to advise on how to do the least damage to trees but the glint of their envy kept showing up at the party instead.

Finally a man with the most onomatopoetic moniker—Buzz—arrived to act as its henchman, and sawed it down—*timber!*

Mourning: one daughter lamented the tiny purple flowers which once pelted the greeny circle of shaded respite, her new bedroom window view lacking the spreading branches, now focused instead on gravel spread by Buzz, my infamous writing shed, the kid version of same, the poke of tenant's ecobus.

Grasp safety and you lose it.

And then bulletholes only confirmed it all.

What marauder so loves
to come at night and
purposely shell us?

No one has seen our intruder: we assumed a man, for no good reason.

I come in the morning to find a resident possum of unknown gender raising his tiny eyes and sharp nose. Dawns mean more loss and a new scattering of holes in the shed, and I am a day late again writing about Roland, who never aimed to do all that much in matters domestic beyond serve mother Henrietta tea.

Imploring letters about the Institute for Roland Studies go unread. Labor unrest knots the supply chain. My ruddy editor sends me a threat louder than the wind hissing through the holes of this text. I owe

an unspeakable
amount of money;
the children need

stability, and this house
will
disappear

from (what is frequently a happy trample, if I failed to mention) our menagerie.

Blue coat and yellow vest

My lady at the bank, the mortgage lady, is a real whiz. A person must admire her; she seems almost not to breathe, mouth half-open, hunched over her calculator, muttering runic strings of numbers, spitting out percentage.

The distance between her competence and mine stays uncrossable: how joyous she is with her late-afternoon careful folders.

I am good with paper, she says, modest in pearls and starched hair. The thing is, I know she will, with that same speed, fire up repossession of our house; how can I meet the mortgage? The underwriters will know loss. I have no job or marriage, no mother or security, and it turns out the shaman has stepped down. My unblood Rick now executes mother's will.

To understand the next step: I already pleaded for more time than the ruddy publisher can allow: his is a small anointed venture; him I also owe.

I had promised three daughters, arrayed on a range of skepticism, that our future would be better, that they might encounter the soul of calm to counterbalance all that had not been.

Labile seas would still, depth could be found in surrender. Leave the known and each day reminds you of ritual sacrifice: *you only get a strong yes when you make a powerful no.*

This axiom I had preached to them so many times—I had put down paintbrushes to become a Roland scholar—and wished to offer our strong yes as something divinely solid rather than whorling sensation, to be someone with an endless capacity for patience, to offer parenthood on tap.

As mentioned, our ecotenant uses the facilities at the local university where he researches protozoa, investigating the motivation for behavior at the level of the cell, but otherwise, self-identified *cathemeral* as he says, sleeps night and often day inside his tilted beige army-camo Luftbus, careening on an angle of stacked two-by-fours, all jutted toward our home.

Do all you can to mark the small
things, to feel your heart
slope leftward, all that
allows gratitude. Raindrop
with hard acid unknown, the frond
of pine scraping your home, dust footprints
winnowing fish downstream in last
daylight. Here will you find the wisdom
of our moment?

Grateful
for the small you(r spirit or soul
or just brain)
become large
as the sky holding all.

Gossip

And so it must be noted that Luft was first to alert me of the danger, noticing so much of what I don't: he first sees the footprints, while I just note clogged gutters.

Someone had tracked near him in the predawn: a large-cloaked homeless woman trundling down the driveway of our cul-de-sac toward the shelter two doors down, the former motel making a village of citizens who now get a room of their own, lending them dignity, maybe a job down the road.

Not a bear, he said.

And yet I could not help but think, in a fit of paranoia, that the figure may have been the ruddy editor to whom I had promised the book on Roland.

Affirmation

As you now know, Roland, born in the fall of 1915, long before he died in a fit of boredom/depression, run over by a laundry truck, was dedicated to his mother Henrietta Binger Barthes.

Having lived with her for sixty years, having had pastry crumbs brushed from his lips by her, having sat with her over coffee, tea, comestibles, Roland took Henrietta's death hard.

When Henrietta died in 1977, her son began writing *Camera Lucida*, a haunted book. Riddled by the exact theory capable of birthing a hundred baby spider plants, including volumes of what one literary pope calls enigmatic realism, the habit of including photos which have an oblique reference to the text.

Known most often to international readers in the work of Sebald, this habit of enigmatic realism has lived in the earlier and later work of untold writers. Quick recipe: include a picture as a form of oblique denotation, a glancing truth off any interpretation gleaned from the text.

Readers of enigmatic realism note the facticity of the photo which, often poorly reproduced, then becomes another portal to lived experience. Either you as reader enter and find yourself in deeper empathy with your author, or stay in uneasy wrestle, since the text had earlier formed different images in your mind's eye.

What does the photo then offer? A chance to alter perception. The linguistic and visual blur or focus a topic but ultimately leave you alone in the room of your reading, the two usually operating more in agreement than mutual understanding. So that when a writer enigmatically includes an image, sans caption, the photo both interrupts and augments (echoes) life in which we never can fully cite where we are as observer-participants.

However, consider the work of a friend, a native cartographer, who resists the inclusion of portraits in order to prevent viewers adjudicating degrees of indigeneity based on such images. Absolute systems constrain vision absolutely. In this case, how clear it becomes: our gaze despoils, our minds warped by the colonial: how to find a place away from such tyranny? Not in the image.

In the case of Roland, he lingers over one photo of his mother as a child, dropped into his midst, his use of aorist here meaning the simple past, the action completed:

I observe with horror, he says, *an anterior future of which death is the stake. By giving me the absolute past of the pose* (aorist), *the photograph tells me death in the future. What pricks me is the discovery of this equivalence. In front of the photograph of my mother as a child, I tell myself: she is going to die: I shudder, like Winnicott's psychotic patient, over a catastrophe which has already occurred. Whether or not the subject is already dead, every photograph is this catastrophe. This punctum, more or less blurred beneath the abundance and the disparity of contemporary photographs, is vividly legible in historical photographs: there is always a defeat of Time in them:* that *is dead and* that *is going to die.*

Roland tells us a photograph is, like some ancient Egyptian funerary object, the living image of a dead thing, always bearing as main elements the studium and punctum. Studium relates to your first attraction to a photo, what makes your eyes wish to stop and engage, an *enthusiastic commitment*, but the punctum interrupts the first with an element of purpose, provoking your questions, the punctum *that accident which pricks me (but also bruises me, is poignant to me).*

Another way to say it: the studium calls out to the part of us most conditioned by historical and cultural experiences.

The Twin Towers.

A handsome rain-shined forest of upstate New York.

A narrow alley of New England.

An arresting light shining off that one particular face.

That which gives us our punctum has to do with our more subjective past: how we have learned to see, layers of more personal (even aleatory) history which compose our vision.

The strange pastness of a photograph, Roland notes, rests in its doubled time signature. An image seems to interrupt an ongoing event yet blends with *presentness* in both the photographer's act of spectatorship and our own when stumbling upon the image.

Elsewhere he says the imperfect tense, in contrast, unlinked with photography, is the *tense of fascination*: the action continues beyond the duration of the words voiced. Examples of the imperfect tense: *I always pined for mother* or *tomorrow we will find some improvement.*

And what Roland appreciates about this form is how it *seems to be alive and yet it doesn't move; imperfect presence, imperfect death; neither oblivion nor resurrection; simply the exhausting lure of memory.*

Mourning will forever stay our act lacking tense. Despite all the attempts to stratify it, grief rejects rungs, strainers, durations, philtrums. For all its taxonomists, grief becomes more like a thick peasant soup with the ladles of the world stirring it, everyone getting a singular portion, each tasting only what they can handle. Mother is mother.

The aorist—the preterite past, in which a simple act is a task fully completed—is one of those forms young Roland loved, and he used it whenever he wrote secretly fawning, pun-riddled letters to his first beloved: a schoolmate named Reybarol, who traveled upward the golden path of the successful educator in the tendentious academy Roland dedicated his life toward tearing down.

Stuck in sanatoria, nursing ill health, unable to amuse himself with city life, young Roland wrote letter after letter to Reybarol, powered by eros and despair. His friend, ascendant, received these pun-riddled gifts, and what did he make of them? Did he understand more of Roland than we do now? Was he the reader who became ideal?

Literature, that extended adolescence: the belief you can still find someone like a first ideal reader.

Say you are stuck far from what you consider life or education, say you find yourself unhealthy, it might become natural that you dedicate yourself to toppling the golden calves you believe live in the far-off center of everything. To imagine a center: an adolescent illusion. To write toward such a center: an aspiration toward maturity. To believe you could be understood: the hope of infancy, our deathbeds, or any life you try to string up between like fancy fairylights. How literature appears to so many of us. How it appeared to Roland, predicting and vanishing, his smile our own Cheshire cat, bemused and ironic between anyone's lines.

Alteration

This editor for the Roland book: I had first met him years ago when we were all so painfully young. Living in Manhattan, I held down three jobs trying to find time to be a Roland scholar. To this editor, I had sent a Roland-inspired story written as a man in love with a younger man. Those first years, before beginning to write on Roland for the dwindling market of those who might understand, I wrote only as an older man.

Why? In my personal life I knew in bed mainly older people—twenty-plus years older, once even forty. My innumeracy one of the innumerable problems that have dogged me. (Cf. problem with timing and history.)

In the first of these stories, I was a Japanese monk in love with a boy at the monastery. In the second, a male model in love with a particular artist at the weekly sitting sessions. Is it of worth to recall why it was so convenient to gender myself male in my early writing?

1) My eyes had been trained to see as a man. (The western canon, which could also mean all the ways a civilization has used to avoid hurt.)
2) My eyes had been trained to see as a man. (Identification with father, which could also mean the formation of a family, created to avoid hurt.)
3) My eyes had been trained to see as a man. (The paucity of women writing around me, despite the flourishing of women emerging elsewhere at that time, keeping central as a performance of labor my parents' workaholism, which stays an epigenetic, immigrant, and capitalist means of avoiding hurt.)

In that precursor time, I envisioned staying with gender hidden, like another, publishing under initials: R.D. Using the dated term—a *tomboy?* What in the swirling patchouli airs of northern California created such assumption? A child, I wished to play endless summertime games of capture-the-flag or horse with my brothers' team of friends, then scrawl observations later, hoping that sight alone would not separate me.

Can a female writer ever fully be inducted into the grotto?

That first grotto crush: a boy who seemed *knowing* in every centimeter of his being: a halo of hair, his neck canted sideways, a soft pelt. Today he grins over social media, a large genial musician, open to collaboration. As children who found themselves undertaking odd habits at the edge of adult peril, the magic rituals of our days a way to decode whatever happened next, we stayed solemn in games under the wingspan of giant birds but indoors found levity, conferred in the unfinished low-ceilinged basement where the dirt of the crawl space suggested dead bodies could be stacked, by a dense iron safe locked with an unknown treasure which no one will ever remove from that house ever, even after my mother's death—there I was almost inducted.

Dirt, rust, mold, concrete, an unknown treasury, plus inclusion in the boys' club: not dissimilar to literature. The possibility that staying by the side of that club, watching and knowing in the present, and recollecting with whatever degree of tranquility, might after all equate with belonging: the writer's dream.

Who came to shine the way? An uncaged bird of an author who spoke at our school, magisterial, her presence so large I recall her as if she were a giant series of lights hung from the roof. Or the female writer whose autofiction tilted on my mother's bedside, a contemporary pioneer wedding prose and prurience, frolicking in something called the Upper West Side with ease so exotic it seemed to spell the writer's life.

I kept bumping into those who kept wishing to yoke writing and conventional femininity: the peer who, in our post-college lives, appeared at a wedding wearing a buxom-bright red dress, claiming she could not be a successful writer as, if you were female, you had to sleep with critics and editors, her concept a ripped thread from some mid-century Hollywood casting couch.

In contrast, I wanted there to be an illuminated scroll we would all write alongside gender, to have writing forever queer the world. Let writing be the way for us to love (without syntagm) friends (the community of our future readers) so we might mate with, as Roland saw it, the *bliss of understanding.*

Because what Roland saw was how all text affects us in two ways: pleasure (*plaisir*) or bliss/orgasm (*jouissance*), which correlate to what he calls readable or writable texts. When you encounter the readerly/readable text, you find pleasure, yet your position as a subject in the center of your own empire does not shift. While what he calls the writable/writerly text offers bliss, a way to explode literary codes and let the reader enter new modes of being, no longer living the false myth of the dominant, subject position.

How do you ever know which text you see? Roland thinks writerly ones matter a bit more, those in which the composition invites you in, those in which you as reader end up connecting with the composition itself so that our codes stay open, streaming through, next to you yet also placing you in a whole nother borough. According to him, take on a readerly text and you stay a staid burgher having tea in your house at your usual hour in your usual armchair. Passive, you receive known pleasures and then shut the book. While Roland would say the writerly text asks for a little effort. Maybe you find yourself enacting some of the actions of the writer to understand the dance out of your usual self, perhaps you become no longer the subject in your armchair, maybe at least one of the codes in the writerly text asks you to alter the very walls of your codes—cultural, hermeneutic, proairetic, semantic, symbolic—all so that you end up in the exact field you might never have guessed before. Your understanding changes the text as it might change you, you have cowritten it, and when you return to it, the book will also have been changed by your future self, you will have rewritten understanding so that reading has the possibility of moving beyond pleasure to become bliss.

In other words, the writerly text is premised on greater optimism about our capacity to change as people—but who's to say?

.

Meetings

The ruddy editor had wanted to meet me in lower Manhattan, in a café which would become significant for every other later meeting, historic only in how memory hungered to layer over it, the palimpsest and signifier awaiting future memories.

I came into the cafe and the light rose in a funnel behind his hair which stacked vertically up toward the skylight. Have you not had that moment in life when phenomena proliferate to signal directions of your future life? In his case, as with others, it was as if heaven's lux finger pointed to say someone would become significant.

You're the first writer I ever wanted to meet, he said, embodying camaraderie. By that logic of encounter, a friendship was born.

More about this editor: he presents to the world a dazzling and breezily associative dismissive mind, not above name-dropping with a kid's glee, as if to say: *hey, I got to go to this party with all the important ones, let's sneak in!* An editor impatient with lesser mortals. Not exactly the kind to come north and skulk around the property shooting at my retooled garden shed as if to create a series of commas on the page. Who has it in for me?

Mature with a cohort and you will see others' eccentricities become more pronounced. In the editor's case, what has grown along with his brilliant expertise is an impatience, neither vicious nor destructive, with those who fail to move through time as he does.

Yet who knows? The game I once loved involved guessing where your opponent placed battleships on a series of coordinates, as you placed yours on a different series, but no longer am I certain, if I ever was, that my inner map has any one-to-one correlation with any outside series of points.

Roland says language holds the necessary yet always illusory hope that you might be able to plot any part of yourself to the outer world. When a marriage rends itself, with children involved, you pilot your course off the gameboard of everyone else's expectations, and then what can you say or believe, what authority do you heed?

Could the bulletpocking come from the person truest to fever dreams but least likely, X who might wish most to mark the distance from first gameboard to current reality? *We were a family,* he keeps saying (had only his actions said the same). Memory of his words: ballistic, x'd out, the dream of the intact.

Unrest

Today the mortgage
official is again after me.
I neglected to sign

something, the disclosure,
federal laws and something else
make her cranky:

I take it personally.
My failure to sustain order.
Try as you might,

forever someone
will be disappointed.
Why is it some women

seem to know how to keep
their physical space so orderly?
I knew you were neglected,

(Vegas mate said). So many mates have
seen this little girl.
You too may find it hard

to hide your most vulnerable self.
The insect grows its carapace
but the soft underbelly remains.

When the genius friend
suggested I do what everyone
often suggests—now

dead, she
gave me a little clay
figurine to imagine my

current self cradling
that elusive inner child—
I could not.

This particular exercise
stays so difficult:
be the adult knowing

how to tend your inner self,
you must know how to attach. Hunger for intimacy,
yet you might also have *disorganized*

attachment style—that great combo
platter of anxiety and avoidance.
You too might wish to please, bearing

the hope of being loved not just for what you
can do, you too might fear
being taken over by the great

tidal wave of others' needs. Believe
others mostly narcissistic, you can find
very little

reason to be proven wrong.
And then there can come the people
who do not

suck all air toward
themselves,
and it is such shock: they stand,

pure in themselves.
(Such is my newish beau.)
Here was the hard dance

for so many years: pining
for connection,
working hard for it, but then afraid

of being engulfed by the others'
fall into the dread pool
where everyone sinks.

I knew myself most fully
when I would stride out, inner soundtrack intact

from that
college beau's little dorm room,

with its great records, teen-boy funk,
crumpled wrappers, burger-and-soda ways.
Out! Into the bracing

cool of another New England
morning. I had known myself fully, I believed,
when sixteen, living with that twenty-six-year-old

beau who lay back in my brother's
room, when closing the door behind
to write a sonnet against the

lure of domesticity.
I would be in bed with him
thinking: okay, now what, how

to make this time matter?
When you are born into
a system in which you feel you must

earn your keep, when you work hard for
love, when you end up with someone
who is one of the most challenging

people to get the love
from, then your system might
go a little haywire.

Back in college, after the burger-and-music
beau, I had a ground-floor
studio apartment

with no bars and no furniture,
occasionally a sea
of clothes on the floor.

One Easter break, two men broke in
when I was there alone. My last
semester. Having seen them,

I ran, inspirited, down the hall.
They took nothing: perhaps
they were high.

Survival itself became a miracle.
When you grow up uncertain where you
begin and others intrude,

violence skirts you. One definition
might serve for both
violence and pride: not seeing

the other and so annexing their being
for your needs. The same semester
of the break-in, I was held

up at knifepoint at night
while ringing a friend's doorbell,
a younger guy who was just

a friend though we lay
together in bed, a guy so raised
on Manhattan mores his speech

about money and power
and his poodle on a science diet
converged: my consolation buddy.

Don't blame us, the woman said,
holding knife at my throat,
we're just motherfuckers.

Don't worry—I said, feeling
odd love, the societal screwup of
it all, probably the pink fog—
I get it, just please if you don't mind
let me have that computer
disk from the backpack,

work mattering more than life
itself, and later at the police
station and driving through

the streets of New Haven, did not wish
to identify her.
Why so silent? the cop asked.

What I believed: the men broke
in because I had not protected my
space, (deserving)(being
not neat enough)(unmothered, not

knowing what to put
into the drawer my mother
had labeled) MISCELLANEOUS.

And the woman held a knife
at my throat because no righteous system
had mothered anyone well yet,

all the greater systems
broken by unlove. What is it about people
who were demonstrably loved by present mothers,

who had enough growing up,
who learned
boundaries, their voices
strong, who know how to
move through the physical world?

My eyes filled with images. Though I
was a painter through most of college,
the faulty dexterity of my

hands protested. All that stapling
of canvases! The caring for the
physical. The order demanded.

. Next to me in class, the future
art-world star crawled with muscle-beach's vaseline
slathered over his careful gym-toned model's

back, readying himself for finicky
curators and the aperture of future
success. You ask yourself

at such moments: how is such exertion
art, how does it solve anyone's
problems, why do the chattering

classes chatter? *What the public wants is*
the image of passion, not passion itself, says Roland, and
also that *the New is not a fashion, it is a value.*

Can we say half of art comes
from anxiety, the other half from play?
Something is missing

in the universe, you feel a hole,
you attempt to patch up your old mud-
house in a new way.

Or you see its beauty and you do
what you can to enter the party.
It is not mere romantic belief

to feel we create art to order

chaos and so head
toward the sublime. The bowerbird
arranges its nonessential art

and mystifies scientists. The infant
makes pattycakes with her
potatoes. Genet loves the smell

of his bespattered bedsheets.
We wish to speak to others,
to touch as we have been
touched, create some kind of
mark: we matter, we mattered.

if you are raised
with the code of loyalty over
autonomy, you will have a different
dance in the workplace,
our contemporary site of passion, (no longer
family, community, religion).

When at work or in life you bump up against people
who do not wish to offer, receive, or ask for help, you will
find your expectations bruised, and it all goes back to that first

family code: loyalty (Old World, interdependence,
easy exchange of favors and help) versus the maverick
code of autonomy (New World, manifest destiny,

self-protection). Roland says:
This is what we are told
by a folk poem which accompanies
these Japanese dolls: Such is life
Falling over seven times
And getting up eight.

All these efforts I have done to create
mother around me:
forever stuck
in labor.

Fall rather than ask for help. Be fuzzy rather than clear.
What does it mean to have a drawer
marked MISCELLANEOUS in your psyche? *Mama*

doesn't struggle with anxiety
like I do, says eldest daughter to my new beau
and to this (regulated as he is) he smiles with the knowing
of my first grotto crush.

Do people well-mothered not
wake with this little bowstring
of nerves? Does the world feel

well-barred, preventing break-ins? Are things less slithery?

Objects flying away.
There is a Giacometti image I love: a man
in a room, every point on the contour of

his being touching a corner of the room.
Which is why it became such a pleasure,
one particular morning before the ripcord,

to rise and have as background
this song of his, one my new beau performed across
the continent the night before—I heard the deadstream,

sonic particles waking me—
his fine grace welcoming everyone, his mention of
snacks at the end, finding myself stirred not just by

the music but by the fact of his ease in
the world, his warm
understanding of what a moment needs.

He too like me learned at some point what it
means to perform to be loved, or what it
means to feel unsafe. And yet

was he born
with a greater birthright of internal ease?
An avatar of love. Yet we have

this emotional congruity, which I first
discovered when we were on a beach,
for a day, he visiting

a scholarly conference with his mother
in California the day before
a brief trip which changed my life—

which made me see the world as having two choices: the technicolor overburdened struggle of those who would make the desert bloom?

Or the void, blessed
by the ancient caryatid with translucent wings, an amethyst head.

Reader, I chose the void.
And then had pleasure emerge.
As if I stumbled into the exact hall of

pleasures that was the inverse of the
marriage. Each time I was sad,
I must have dropped a tinsel

coin into the future that now became mine.
And then what do you reach for?

Intimacy

In lonely years, married, when everyone else seemed to be in love or loving or just feeling good, when pop songs and celebrities seemed like Greek gods frolicking in an empyrean I would never reach, I must have subscribed somewhere to something which ended up meaning that I got the sex email newsletter of someone I will call Rafina. While I blocked her, I somehow still get her exhortations. She traffics in grandly nurturant carnality: *Darling! Sugar! I just had the most explosive Orgasm with Jimbo.* The lovable aspect of the benign narcissist.

Rafina is filled with herself, confiding in her ideal audience as her waist does this little figure-eight dance while she tells us how to lead the embodied life, supporting herself with an odd striptease of intimacy from the tropical island of explosion on which she seems to live. She could be from Germany or Suriname, but what is constant is her self-regard, well performed, clearly a lucrative business: her missives enter my email box with a regular orgasm of self-revelation which our time might encourage (and which I fear this text, *jouissant* or not, becoming.) What does her young son think? We live in the time of such exhortation toward intimacy, and I am not immune to what Roland would call such Values.

They have become my shield
even as I hope to bring the loved one
(of art) near, our greater story about art
(love) nearest of all.

And Jonathan said to David, go peacefully, given how much we have both sworn within
the name of mysterious creation, saying our bond will forever stretch between the two of us,
between our two lines forever. And he rose and left for the realm of all busy labor.

Clouds

A story you need
to tell means you
are not apologizing
for existing.

In the weekly heir calls in which you find yourselves reenacting the family dynamic, you find yourself resorting to the greatest trick: the great invisibility act of your childhood. If you were invisible, you couldn't be bullied. And so you don't speak and when you do it is a rush of words, tight and maybe wiry and over-caffeinated, because you don't want to take up more than your due and the longer you're in the open air, the more likely your neck will be throttled or at least false stories will be projected upon you. *He is an older uncle,* says someone, as if that explains Uncle Rick. But you have friends who are older uncles who do not take up space with the same entitlement.

What is your survival brain trying to protect by obsessing or judging? Fear or need. The fear of being squashed. The need to stay safe. Judging, you create bad magic, as in a fairytale tower's fence of vines sprung up around the self.

If you were on your deathbed, what would you want to have been your legacy? Connection, love, service, generosity, great works of art that moved people to think or see or feel or be able to articulate differently.

But why differently? The rock tumbles into the river and so the course of the river is altered. Does alteration matter?

And yet how tired you are, as if
pregnant for the first time with a new self.

Why

Roland lists modes of waking: *sad, wracked (with tenderness), affectless, innocent, panic-stricken.* For a time, I wake each morning with my mind rehearsing argument with X, who found one part of life spark in being a contrarian.

Oppositional defiance disorder finds life-force in argument, and can be carried by genes. Much easier to offer diagnosis than empathy, both a means of returning toward respect. You can feel for the situation that caused X to suffer, traumatic brain injury as a child or when a casino bouncer, or perhaps all that his genes carry. How much you would like to stay open-hearted.

All meditations tell one to rest easy in the great embrace, but when dissociation has been your bedmate, you wake to the great O of absence you cannot fill: what is missing, as Germans would say, *was ist los?*

How many ways have I failed to provide a safe home? Is it impossible? No writing shed ever really finished in which to finish this book on Roland that will never be written. No safety. A polite temporary tenant who turned out to be a drug dealer. Our ecotenant, the trees with thick branches that wish to fall on our roof, such anthropocene problems.

Where was my first mistake?

Show me whom to desire

Now I am with the person who forever questions conventional assignations: self, other, world, gender, parenthood, redemption.

Every time I assign a role, he riddles it.

Why was whoever I have been always working? That person was escaping (toward another future in which work was not required) or burning out (hocked by the past for the future.) Both scenarios create a huge helium balloon of the self. You imagine the self as being someone who will survive better if you just work a little harder.

The same is true with these binary definitions: man/woman—in a relationship/out of it.

And yet when you leave a relationship, to yourself, to your former mate, to your former ideas of overwork, the demon you must face is your own dependency on the former constructions.

Why is working hard such a sanctioned part of our current consciousness? Because on one particular continent, a few believed in manifest destiny: never rest, tame the outside world, let inner grace be revealed by the extent to which you splay yourself over the outer!

Work hard and avoid your inner caverns. Imagine everyone is so endlessly dependent on you, your life feels as if it might become (only) that of giving to others. Give up your own gameboard and wonder why you are playing at all.

After the break-in and knife-to-the-throat incidents, of all people Rick, so frequently wise, there's the rub, said: *Take greater precautions* as he had taught me so well *you need to recall the body deserves care because without your body your soul has no vessel.*

Your spirit needs your body intact. Do most of us need reminders to recall the body deserves care enough to hold spirit? When one daughter is upset, she sings the praises of dissociation, but finds it odd that her mind then attacks her body. The center can only sometimes hold.

Ravishment

Roland spoke of spirit moving through body with such rapture: in a new relationship, *neither knows the other yet. Hence they must tell each other: 'This is what I am.' This is narrative bliss, the kind which both fulfills and delays knowledge, in a word, restarts it. In the amorous encounter, I keep rebounding—I am light.*

In America in the 1920s, the movement called meliorism had people chanting this mantram every day:

every day in every way I get better and better.

Reroute the brain and all is better. But if you find it hard to surrender the concept of yourself as an asylum seeker in the land of love, a love refugee, do you have this choice? (And in the background plays music about glacial music, not unlike newish beau's, making the question itself a joke.)

This music that beau cares about suggests that our main truth rests in slowness, a view of prehistory and later apocalypse. That we may attend to the small gritty data of our living. We may care for the samsara in which our monkeyminds like to frolic. We do well to attend each vine and vein in every leaf while at the same time knowing how mountains see beyond us.

And so in the speed of my messy room with the cabinet that does not work, which beau said I just had to bang shut, I try to see the glacial movements of this moment, to arrive, to choose this state.

The happiest older women I know, even concentration camp survivors, call their state of mind a choice. Each has said to me, in so many ways: you must make the choice of happiness, you must savor the strawberry. They swivel their hard-working hips when music comes on, they feel ravished by the joy of the unexpected visitor.

Many non-huckster preachers will say our problem is we always strive: that it is good just to note *arriving*, *arrival*, *arrived*. To bask in this moment now. My dear friend who struggles in her long marriage says she has learned such savoring to be the key to sexuality. She strives to do all she can to cherish the good, focus on it, expand it, dilate it, let it be everything. *Simulatedt*: the typo a visual poem. Bring everything inside, you might find the good.

Yet some of us experience the greatest stress in sameness, and novelty becomes the precipice over which we hurl ourselves with abandon, some genetic latticework making us heed most acutely the risk of new pleasure.

The problem with the routine of cleaning one's room is that while order may be a mother, it is not the evolutionary focus of vitality unless one anoints the act with the concept of love which is always self-renewing, as if one could be Roland's lover importuning him for the first time.

I hate cleaning my room, middle daughter says, *it is an act which leaves me terrified and my existence emptied.* Once I cleaned youngest daughter's room so thoroughly and she came back to say: *I don't know myself, I am lost.* And proceeded to mess it up again in exactly the way that made her know herself best within a friendly animal den.

The Californian mystics
would say: *imbue*
the act of cleaning with
attention.

When Vegas mate and I were trying to have our children *nest*—to stay in the same old house while the separating/divorcing parents moved in and out—I came distressed into the mess of the old home, as if finding another robbers' break-in of the house, as if finding all they had smashed and left lying about, and spent two full days cleaning our communal nest. How not to resent their father? How to do it with love?

A friend said: call it a new contract. *With this act, I am freeing myself of the old contract, I am thanking the world, I am beginning afresh, I am loving my children, I am creating a space for the new peace we will all know.* Could this be the new ritual sacrifice? Abandon the inner skeptic. Chant and intone intention. Let the old acts configure themselves on a new gameboard: trust the banality of the act, take a new journey, spell yourself anew.

Encounter

The oddest part of finding another person's
sexuality after years of having been with a different person
is that it is like a garden with a wholly different door and key,
as if one were indeed Alice having fallen.

You see that, ah, they like to linger under this mushroom
and then they like to suddenly take flight after this toadstool
and then you are sitting at a long table
and prating about this and that which really has nothing to do
with anything allowed at any former table,
and in fact the table is not even a table as such,
it is floating over Towsley Canyon near Los Angeles, hovering,
and then you see two deer stop and eye you
as if they understand who you are in the great mating dance,
you feel a part of nature with this person in
the way that X, though a nature-lover, was more
a part of cities.

But then there is this to remember:
your newer love, you rode behind him on
a bicycle in Berlin at night, a city he knew,
watching his back, and you knew you had arrived
somewhere you had not even dreamed possible.

It is not that long misery creates joy.

Of course there had been joy in the marriage, and by
declaring annulment, it was as if
you acceded to some master narrative
which said *yes, there was no joy, now this is the new script—*
yet as psychologists say, you script your life anew.

But this thing that happened back before our ripcord quarantine,
doing yoga in an overheated bedroom at the parsonage,
when suddenly a part of my body
looked as unfamiliar to me, newly loved,
as new as the concept of a crested butte—
what is a crested butte anyway?—this is what has
started to happen now too. You are re-
membering parts of yourself, bringing them back into
the newly constellated twinkle
-fingered family of being and finding
a fresh clan moves in fresh ways.

And then time will not stop its march,
it keeps on.

Annulment

Introductions frame our hearing,
such simple profundity lives in how we meet anyone.

This light is what we look for in
marriage and love and even divorce:
to recall the cosmic stardust hope
inside all introduction.

When living in New York,
determined not to couple
with the man who became Vegas mate,
as mentioned, I organized radical picnic parties
on the Upper West Side
getting to live with only some friction the
fiction of being a Roland writer
during which huge platters of lemon
-bedecked roast vegetables
were on offer (foods of ritual sacrifice)
and there I introduced the one
whom I believed would not become (my Vegas) mate
to young lissome friends of my acquaintance
until an older strawberry-savoring friend, yet another dead this year, said
(one of several to whom I introduced X,
before leaving that friendship
so that he could feel freer to curse about me)
What about him? Why not him?

And it was true: I laughed,
X's values were wonderful,
I knew he would be interested,
passionate, funny, and loyal
forever, whatever that meant,
plus he walked straight out
of the book of Paley.

I bring ease to noxious kitchens
and fuming bedrooms,
Paley says, carnal as ever,
one of her characters
speaking that dialect
no one understands out west.
People who have tried to live
by cross-ventilation alone have thanked me.

The problems began
when he and I could no longer
hear the other's yearning.

Askesis

Divortere: to turn toward
other paths.

Askesis: *severe self-discipline, usually for religious reasons.* These two might seem to war, but here shall we try to combine them? In one of the oldest codified laws on divorce, some 1760 years before the common era back in Babylon, the king Hammurabi himself, allegedly, carved the first law on divorce into a massive black finger-shaped stone stele with some 281 other laws.

Say you were a man wishing to unravel: a simple verbal utterance sundered the union: *You are not my wife.* The man was then to pay a fine and return the dowry. The wife, however, had to file a complaint to obtain rupture.

Let what I write here not be reproach—that tribunal already filed in diaries—but rather, in a movement toward self-discipline, a path toward light, perhaps of use for others.

To say it straight as I can: an infective agent shot in, vigorous and bristling with possibilities of transmission. Aiming to create a daughter haven, I failed to understand the news. My newish love jumped onto a plane in March and showed up, hooded and ready to engage in the float of an imagined two-week quarantine, as if of the family. Careful, of stately cadence, but alert. So began our cohabitation.

Everything was proving untenable; great horrors mauled the world; as in certain island-nations oppressed by political regimes, the ravaging brought out, with unpredictable rhythm, the angel or devil in the populace; and meanwhile the Institute for Roland Studies slowly sank with a few bubbles of distress, my ruddy editor and his publishing house also hocking themselves to bits.

Uncoupling distracted me, a hook sunk deep in the emotive-connective tissue. How is it we keep worrying the scar tissue? How do we get so addicted to the smallness of the personal sting? I kept revisiting scenes of former yokage. And tried neither to recreate nor natter on about them. Waking flung from dreams, still rehearsing arguments with X, the jejune ego forever seeking to be right.

And every now and then X, isolated, threw one of his tantrums, making everyone unhappy—o, sad recall of his own father's thin-lipped smile whenever he had thrown a line with enough sadism to sting son most, getting a rise out of him. X could not flee the habit, occasionally doing whatever he could to hurl flames into the new home. My task stayed to focus on the good, to avoid engagement as in a reverse courtship.

Yet still, as if a child, I would freeze, flooded, wishing to fawn: as if a child with bullies or Rick. Disbelieving: how could someone be like *that*? Didn't he want our kids to have a more peaceable life? Had he not heard a thing in the parenthood classes about avoiding making them weapons? Wasn't the world better? Didn't he mean better? How could he accept this meanness when it arose in himself? Overhearing him speaking to a daughter: *you can tell your goddamn mother I saw her note.* But his moods and impulses had semi-predictable cycle, and here lived the rub: no gnostic binaries of good/evil separated him from the rest of humanity; he had his good days.

Seeing in him any quality meant I was forced to see the same in myself: Vegas mate and his toddler swagger in a dark mirror. And here I have written myself into a corner.

Having bitten off more than you can chew, so goes the saying, but chewing more than you can bite stays our more common habit. People outside the culture industry don't always understand how very flimsy are the joists that hold up the house for writers and opiners. Hope to keep the warmth going for newly built family through a cold New England winter with fires stoked, no manuscripts burnt yet, yet the furnace grows impatient, rocking its metal feet.

Consider the premise of the womb: some rush out, others fight to stay in a bit longer like my three daughters, who rejected their first zone of uncertainty: thresholds have never been their friends.

Emerging into the unknown, this period of catastrophe requires this negative capability from all of us: accepting unhinging and continuing to believe in the illusion of the firm. (Is it any mistake that the firmament, a heaven, is made of sky and unreachable?)

Some Buddhists say the chance of being born into a human incarnation is equivalent to the probability of a sea a sea turtle rising from ancient watery depths into a small golden yoke randomly placed on the surface of the water: so lucky to be born human!

And so too you could recognize: we are so lucky to have all landed here, to be on this journey together. Your new love does not believe in reincarnation but when pressed will say he might have been a raccoon, big patient eyes, active hands. Or a hard-working mother of the Levant with ten children, who, when labors are done, goes to a nearby hillock to wonder at the night sky.

When it comes to thresholds: who are you? How do you play it out? How to make this moment's crossing toward a new path illumined as a beautiful scimitar curved under the moon?

Leaving the small Chinese-goods grocery, let us say you find two masked girls emerging from the next-door establishment. You might be struck by the way they investigate the backs of their hands, as if to see a moon reflected, as one does in the ancient astrolabe ritual closing the sabbath, when one aims to see the braided candle's flame reflected in one's nails, the grand in the small particular. Any of us might hope to see our future in the now.

But no. Their moment's deep intent study has to do with this simple truth: they just got their nails done, luminescent pearly white, French tips, a particular act of self-grooming which brings some joy: two caught, deeply caring, in a parallel so tight it almost spells perfection. Firmament: *the apparent surface of the imaginary sphere on which celestial bodies appear to be projected.* No amount of self-discipline can get you there. Is it possible to train your mind to dwell only on the beauty of what is before you? Your three daughters and beau eating cauliflower curry soup together on a night in which the house is warm enough: could such a moment of domestic bliss be enough?

Reverberation

Some twenty-two centuries after Hammurabi, X and I had our working out of an agreement toward divorce, led up to in intermittent sessions with one acute mediator, our lawyer with her forehead broad and mouth quirked at the exact angle to contain all human foible.

Though I come from salt-miners, no ancestor could have poured more salt into the wound. Still I commend to anyone who needs it such collaborative sundering: the one-lawyer divorce.

That lawyer with her quick mind and searchlight clarity! Despite the mire of picayune detail, she led us, wading through and beyond.

And so we were not exactly free from the fireweed and thornbush of human interaction but got to glimpse a tiny clearing ahead.

In the caste system of modern life, exactly what regal temperament or dint of birth qualifies someone to be a divorce mediator? Can you imagine yourself waking with buoyant step each day and bearing fresh soap, stepping into a shower, only to emerge clean and ready to sit in closed rooms with your share of couples disentangling, each with their own inner mustering, their own scales for war and peace?

In 1519, young Martin Luther began writing on marriage, only a year or so after he had pinned his Ninety-five Theses on the Wittenberg church door, his version of Hammurabi's carved 282. When he began his revolutionary writings on coupling, Luther argued that marriage should be for love and companionship as well as for procreation and that it is, for most people, a better choice than celibacy.

What I first understood from scholars and believed notable: it took Luther three years of being married to begin writing about divorce; you could say *sola scriptura* flowed from *sole fide*.

Yet my ruddy editor, well-partnered, happened to believe the exact opposite: that it took Luther three years after starting to write of divorce to sacrifice celibacy, wed, and by most accounts go on to live the life of a happy husband.

Who errs? I turned toward an early divorce in the American colonies: 1650, Herodias Long, a wonderfully wayward woman notorious for fierce self-advocacy—perhaps you have met her heirs—bearing an entitlement both geographic and emotional. But when is geography not emotional? (When you have dissociated long enough from the earth.)

Some say the peculiarity of American marriage and divorce springs from the way Luther's heirs turned marriage from sacrament to contract, regulated by magistrate rather than priest. If historians no longer consider the Reformation the hinge on which history turned, nonetheless something protestant tinged the New England springtime day we banished sentiment, a cool legal asperity marking release from our life together.

We were losing
something. To declare
an end will always be
artificial. Of course
memory and grief will always
know a particular
eternity.

To have realized all those years ago, in our first five minutes of meeting, that history had conspired against us, that each was never meant to be—forget my mother's use of Ivory soap to prevent my existence as her second child, it was also true that both our fathers were born in a small Australian outback town, some years apart, which meant those ready to hoist our families by apocryphal horns had failed. Both families contained, removed, and murdered in this century, the last century and even before, yet somehow no circumstance could slay whatever led to our standing in line at a convenience store in a campus town, our first meeting, his two hot dogs for a dollar, my huge ice coffee for the same, and then our later walk within that dripping summer which led to an outdoor New England lurid-green concert because we seemed to have a friend in common. So it began.

Cosmic destiny, Vegas mate would later say. We were not supposed to have met and borne these children, our ancestors defying all history of aggression, yet our three grew under our yoke of struggle, in rancor-laced cheer, as if we all remained in prior centuries, as if all had not been blasted into our ostensibly new world.

You fulfilled your old-world karma with him, says my friend the buddhist, *you burnt off the peasant, prisoner, pogrom karma.*

Whatever magic the broad-faced divorce lawyer managed to apply led to the cold puritan day outside an actual court building. Compliant as our slain forebears, we lined up with others ready for an odd moment of community. Sentiment flourished. Hoping to hold on to a vision of our future lives in which our family lived out its happier twinkly-fingered new constellation, I gave Vegas mate my own little eulogy, a page from a legal pad, speckled with praise, apology, remorse. As if we would never speak again. And in return, later, he gave me a scrap, a hasty epitaph with scabbed letters saying something of touching simplicity, to this effect:

> *R.D., sorry I spoke about you so badly*
> *always to our daughters and everywhere to everyone else.*

This apology contained a legion of misfired speech, our arguments, the way I publicly became the butt of his jokes, in the vein of that midcentury comedian's line: *take my wife, please.* I appreciated the note all the more when, soon after our unraveling, I gave a few lectures on Roland around the States and one by one people came up to me after each and said—after the first time, it became less shocking: *thank god you're not with him, X always talked so badly about you to everyone, complained of you, sucked air out of every room, never understood why you were with a narcissist who made everything about himself—he blamed you for his life.* In protest, my psyche shot up holographic scenes of his tenderness, the burred mournful palpation of his being, and that his brain probably could not control the way his 1950s-imprinted era and father's temper had left such watermarks on him. *Just because someone is kind to you some of the time, that's not enough—you want a mate who is always kind,* said a friend, seeing my younger self unfettered and joyous in those early mud-caked honeymoonish photos.

Of those photos, Roland would say I participated in the code of appearing to be the beloved. When are we ever free of such codes? You reading this also wish to belong to a code: the reader is beloved, the lover, the one who seeks love. How do we escape them? Why do we always fall blind to the codes of others and believe we are creating our own way of being, a strange legacy of our individualistic time?

Back in the hallway of divorce court, awaiting our turn inside, X and I sat on hard wooden benches as if out on a date, joking (a moment in which we were kind). A short bald man left a room, still arguing with his tall orange-haired ex-wife. We would not be those people, no, not the Lockhorns, that forever-fighting couple with the scary horrible square chins from my childhood's Sunday comics. Whoever they were, we would not be them. We would observe decorum. So much of marriage orients toward twin polestars, good faith and right effort, and toward these, in our last moment, we aimed.

Until entering a courtroom made of women. Until hearing the utter narrowing-in toward the one question, asked by the female judge whose reputation had called her an ethical dealer.

Are you sure she asked us—the last time we would be us *beyond any reasonable doubt* we both shifted *are you sure that you have worked and tried every last thing*

Imagine! every last thing?

to keep this marriage alive?

When in life have you known that you have done every last thing to keep something alive?

In that room of women, I teared up. Could that be an answer? The unmothered, hardest-working part of me had chosen an unmothering, hard-working marriage.

Overwork at the marriage and in the world as a twisted means of mothering the outside and the self: such had been my prayer of nonserenity.

Reader, in that courtroom, whatever I had been: I did dissolve.

The incommensurability of inner reality welled up against the limits of speech: what can one never say? Would love always be work? Would love work out for any of us, all of us?

That this courtroom happened to be in New England, in the biggest cobblestoned town closest to the country green of our first outing, o drippy outdoor first-date summer concert, the upstate country to which New Yorkers must escape, how mimsy were those borrowed groves, the life of easeful love a grove ending up not ours. The geographic proximity almost coincidental. We ended up where we began; the serpent swallowed its tail but the cycle would not end, not yet.

We returned to this town towing third daughter. Anything but Vegas stayed an adopted rural realm where Vegas mate never felt at home, as he said, too far from his own birth paradise, too far from any real city.

Roland would appreciate the way Vegas codes had helped Vegas mate: he had grown up in the big-spending tuxedo'd-waiter city of the fifties and after, the remaking of the town in which people spoke in a way that made his own way of speaking make sense. His mother a nurturing lipsticked waitress, his father a blackjack dealer turned pawnbroker, he could not help it, he said, his life filled with brusqueness and the limiting views which justify it; it has been documented that even pigeons squawk more quickly in Vegas.

While the trees of New England host slim trees and hardy birds: new-growth forest, host to long-ago timber homes and woodfires, a long history of settlers, appropriators, colonialists, murderers, councilmen, puritans, reparative ventures. On bad days, raising three girls, Roland studies on the wane, and mate losing truck-driving jobs due to the entropy of rage or rage from entropy, our landscape looked bleak.

I had to (re)learn to love the nature here, glacial waterfalls spilling into ponds and old granite, mossfairy landscapes, secret grottos in which to find life.

The judge ejected us out: divorced. Out into nature. We were to tend our young now separately. And in the state of Massachusetts, a legacy of Hammurabi's Code, the bureaucracy asked us to learn parenthood: a weekly class we each were to take separately, as, without tutelage, we might continue our trend of failure.

Nights, I drove to a hospital to learn how to be a parent. One daughter was seventeen, another fifteen, the other eleven. Passing the amplified heartbeats of the ward for those prematurely born, the NICU, I found my way to a conference room for those prematurely divorced, a ward in which to hear my brethren sing distress.

Right now such a class might be taking place. There you will find the angriest of the sunderers, jaws set hard toward ego's north, half-listening to legalities, more bloated with righteousness than the cheeky squirrels of my poorly tended garden, beings so ready to pounce on the last little bit of tomato clinging to the vine: their goal being to confirm not only parental rights but ultimate rightness. As if such rightness exists.

My ex was always a nightmare jawsetters say, *ex as a parent is worse.* The tenet they live by has the unforgiving logic of a hearse: slam shut all sentiment. Yet treat buried love untenderly and it might wake, zombie-like, to plague you. I tell myself this even as I put these words down. How the jawsetters raised hands and lamented to enlist others in grievance, no matter how petty or grand, far too heavy to carry alone: *what do you do when someone is a jerk about transitions?*

Vegas mate could not be called a bad father: just prone to an impulsive scary fury he never recalled, staying disorganized, muddling others but defiant, looking for umbrage and insult. His mother used to say to him: why so nervous? As if a creed, he foreswore so many forms of calm communication others swear by, staying committed for years to unemployment while using the kids as his excuse without our agreement, while I would have been willing to stay home (the good-enough mother), not having to work several jobs to support all of us. Once I helped him get a job teaching mechanics at a local community college but soon they fired him for his anger and he seemed happy again, excelling in edging me out of the home. He finally got a new license and took on the habit of being the driver on call, getting calls at three in the morning, end-result being I could never organize time with daughters between catching moments to work on Roland.

Often these days, with my daughters around town I run into strangers who say, on hearing a kid's name: *O,* you're *the ex-wife, I don't know your ex-husband well but you're so-and-so's mother, yes, I heard about you from him* eyes widening to hold the ire of his words. Use of the perfect and imperfect tense: despite the apology note he gave me at divorce court, he could never stop talking.

Substitute truck-driver, X loved how the emergency of the job sparked the house. Called for deliveries out of nowhere, he loped out for a haul as if a happy martyr for the cause, though he only made some fifteen dollars an hour. Supply chain faltered, labor protested, raises happened, he was called and became important. Any conversation about it turned into bullying tantrums. All of us learned quite well to jump and shy away. *Look, father works!* His loyalty never up for question, just the intermittency of the work ethic. The state of Massachusetts had a point, asking us to pause and reconsider: *what did you mean, daring to be two mammals raising your young? Consider history before you officially break for the future.* Clearly we had fumbled some part of our storyline.

Crucial points from that parenthood class: *always speak kindly of the other parent; support the other's way.* Acronyms bandied about included recalling the STUG, a *spontaneous traumatic upswelling of grief*: a sine wave cycling, a miscarriage of the dream.

This grief cycle (they promised) would shorten. Equipped with the acronym STUG, I knew the following: one steady-eyed barista watched me tear up, unable to finish our small talk when the particular incantation came on as backdrop: *I want to see you dance again,* sings Neil.

This song above all had been ours: despite sadness, Neil sings, there could be return. So many grief cycles live forever (within and) after a long marriage.

What I learned, and wish to give to others: when attached to anyone over any haul, you must be aware of every single moment you start to secret parts of yourself away for protection. To make things work, the American phrase, you must find instead a way to share the very questions that make you wish to hide. (The much-quoted Winnicott quotation of our time: *it is a joy to be hidden, and a disaster not to be found.*) Once too much of you is hidden away from your partner, attachment has no place to land. You start living a parallel life, your authentic self no longer in conversation, your relation loses both magic and glue, abandoning the possibility of being seen and growing.

The key to intimacy:
stay on the journey together,
show the wound
yet only to the safest.

You get hurt as a child. Someone is never there, someone pierces you. The hippocampus easily confuses details and context, leaving you with a welter of pain. In that ocean, your memory tries creating a legible story: cause and correlation. The more you repeat it, the deeper the track grows. Neurons that fire together wire together. Later, you find yourself angry, hurt, or disappointed, and this dragon from your amygdala awakes to return, vast and hungry.

We are here to help one another heal, says the genius friend, *we share the journey, in a safe bond we move toward a partner, and in the light of current love, all wounds are healed.*

Or time wounds all heels, as the sorry adage goes, and mine had worn out pursuing the possibility of safe attachment in the marriage. No longer enough left in me to believe it existed. So much of me had been secreted away, I could find no landing spot.

Open as a flower, soon into childhood I learned to close; then I performed and worked hard toward recapturing the bliss of that openness. Our marriage had acted as a homunculus, a wizened being with its own needs in which we lived—some a priori dictates made by a mad maker. He too suffered. We all know this risk: a child self can shrivel away.

No one spoke: the host, the guest, the white chrysanthemums

At one point in the disentanglement, I ran into them, youngest daughter's teacher and her husband, on a Sunday morning at the market after they had gone to church. Adopted at birth, she felt keenly the growing pains of her elementary charges: clearly an enlightened mother of four grown children.

Remarkable to me still: the regard in which her husband held her—when you lack, others can seem irradiated by abundance. Surely over the years there had been so many parents who had approached her, so many times he stood by as small talk was exchanged. The cast of his patient embracing light on her startled me, a living punctum. The beautiful embrace of his love-light around her, protective and yet offering space. He needed no entry; he was there to support. How incredible to see that gift of intimate autonomy in a(nother) couple.

The grief carried in one line of the song, the one that made me tear up before the barista, was based on shifted tectonic plates (the past swallowed the present). There could be no more dancing again, the verb tense and duration proved impossible. Grief has no compartment; there had never been a husband who could hold all our future ruptures; the husband I recalled seemed to care mainly for his own sentiment in relation to whether or not I ever danced with him again.

The ongoing lesson of adulthood: inside personal relationship, your emotions and experience are yours to handle. Terra incognita I had traveled thirsty and ravenous, trying to be a steadying presence, feet firm, ready to play and console, to support and confirm, to model—like the former teacher—some different possibility about love for some luminous children who still knew how to skip so lightly forward, filled with wonder at each day. On the wheel of feelings, is wonder the true antonym of grief?

Renewal

I want to see you dance again
on this harvest moon
(sings Neil).

Why? Can we return to it? Why does the singer want to see the addressed dance again? To remember that first tendril of tenderness that led them toward each other.

There will be replenishing, claims the song. The harvest is a cycle, a season, all comes back.

Some earth had turned, new tendrils poked up, and the tiniest part of me was curious, like a ladybug new to spring, landed inside but exploring a windowsill, curious about light and nourishment as well as what in that world outside could ever be safe?

Our new age favors the image of the spiral to chart people's growth (and perhaps as in this treatise, in art): we find ourselves ascending, and yet certain points of the circle resemble a similar point of lower stratum.

I propose we recall that field of object relations Winnicott helped create. Object relations says our first sense of self is formed in attachment to a primary caregiver—say, a mother—to an internalized mother who acts as a stable referent for all else that follows. There can also be an understanding of parts, such as, say, the *good breast* that feeds, while the starved infant who finds nothing lives in relation to the *bad breast.*

Young Donald Winnicott, the child of an ostensibly happy and fortunate family, saw himself as being oppressed by two sisters and the dark moods of his mother. One day, he would speak of trying to *make his living by keeping his mother alive.* His own problems came from not knowing where to pocket his own habit of performative *goodness*, something he had taken on in trying to lift mother's mood. We can be grateful for the insights that rise from such a habit.

The ingredients of your life can create joy, a friend of mine wrote on a postcard to me this past year.

You look at DW and, with the clarity of retrospect, see how habits were sown; the wounded healer always bears the most passion; later he made his living working with troubled youth. *Only the true self can be creative and only the true self can feel real,* exclaims DW. If you have play with a mother who responds, in some ideal situation, your instinct for play (creativity, authenticity) is aroused. What happens when you lack such a holding environment? What do you recreate?

Expenditure

Roland says the modern writer can only mimic *a gesture forever anterior, never original* and is forever layering whatever has been done over itself, yet the *Author-Gods,* those early originals, have their bond clear: *the same relation of antecedence a father maintains with his child.* When those Author-Gods write, according to Roland, they are *born simultaneously* with the text. There is for them no other time *than that of the utterance, and every text is eternally written here and now.*

Yet as I felt—

raised in a particular town after a surge of romanticism had found its snubnose paper-airplane destiny, as every generation feels, including these kids I try to help raise—

we skid into the present moment already late, coming after the fact, we find ourselves speaking with tongues of the past, wondering if they are our own: *the key to a text is not to be found in its origin but in its destination.*

Or as Kahlil Gibran intoned from everyone's bookshelf in that era: your children are not your children!

They are the sons and daughters of Life's longing for itself

and later

You are the bows from which your children as living arrows are sent forth.
The archer sees the mark upon the path of the infinite, and He bends you with His might that His arrows may go swift and far.
Let your bending in the archer's hand be for gladness;
For even as He loves the arrow that flies, so He loves also the bow that is stable.

Try to create any text, even your life, even your life as a decent parent, even your life as a decent parent to a book on Roland you must write in order to be a good parent to children fleeing your ideas of them even as you fled the marriage codicil, and you are no longer that author sitting and offering any ultimate meaning.

What Roland says: the Author-God is dead, the text flees its creator, and only the tissue of meaning rests in the passions and understanding of readers. The deity's life illumines the text written by the scriptor, bearing the exact same *relation of antecedence a father maintains with his child,* the struggle nothing less than Oedipal: the *birth of the reader must be at the cost of the death of the Author!*

In other words, Roland forever argues against the criticism in which the background of the author offers some ultimate explanation of the text: none exists. In his view, if you give a text an author and force upon it a single interpretation, you impose a limit, based on your own codes, and anyway, that text itself is more like *a fabric of quotations.*

You may be reading these words and understanding what Roland means when he says all work is *eternally written here and now* each time you read because the *origin* of all meaning lives only in *language itself.* Such recognition might help you or also seem obvious, reader, but for me Roland was the revolution I sought to heed:

decenter the family (or literature) so that no longer did we have to obey any absolute authority but the call to be present in each moment of reading life (or any other text). You exist as many beings, understood in so many other ways. And none of us can fully be the Author-God of our own life; we write life by reading it.

Once I thought Roland to be alone in his absolutist declarations of relativism, but he is not. The Buddhism of Sri Lanka, Theravada Buddhism, which some find a fiercer and less hospitable discipline, has an idea not unrelated to Roland's ideas about text. Contingent dependency and anicca, the no-soul doctrine of karma, mean that no one soul survives all your lives, but rather gets distributed as bits of cosmic fluff in the ether, which means that everything you do always affects everyone else's merit and salvation. Born, you enter a giant invisible web of connection that sees beyond time.

A belief which seems enacted in the new love's confrères, an ensemble of well-trained composer-musicians committed to improvisation. So notable how they deal with the bodies of others. In rehearsal sessions, they move like dust motes, authored only by Brownian motion, sacrificing authorship for improvisation within parameters.

Imagine you sit watching them in a glass-walled room with forest beyond. How rigorously they both abandon and claim authorship. Each player has navigated shoals of childhood discipline or lack, alphabets of forbidding or forgiving mentors, lexicons of awards or deserts, but no matter, their well-practiced spines are called to the moment in which they offer a note to the universe of the ensemble, erect and alert when heading into performance.

Such good players and translators that, when they are done making music and sidle near one another, a faux casualness veils them, bearing an aura of performance even when smearing peanut butter on a rice cake at the communal table. Because they are aware of the slipperiness of any musical entry into the collective, when they speak even to joke, they still seem more incarnated, simultaneously taking on and shucking authorship.

To say it straight, reader, since clearly I am enamored: some good faith pulses through them. They know what it is to listen to others. And what elegant mercy new love shows in magnetizing all of them and their work.

When the musicians return from peanut butter to practice his new piece, all timbrels and drone, your mate's dance before them as he conducts is loose-limbed, a person trusting the fulfillment of some collective destiny. *Can you start conducting a few bars earlier?* the oboist asks more than once, since clearly beau's trust itself wishes to conduct.

You notice that, unlike a herd of writers—the idea most often an oxymoron—these musicians treat one another's foibles with the respect of bodies in space deserving gentleness, that soft tier of love extra yet necessary like music itself which is also exactly the laughter our universe needs.

Could you admire anyone more?

In these last months, you and new love have found a separate occasional and temporary dwelling for him, to lessen the cohabitation friction known by younger daughter. You go for a drizzly mushroom walk on the path nearby, the fungi of a variety you have never known, the frolicsome spray of tiny white niblets like seafoam over plastered leaves in a high cathedral forest, the wild purple nubs and blushing pink open slatternly mushrooms, the empurpled brown flowers and white vertical coral, the huge cheese-covered pancakes and bialy fungi, or the extreme amber frills of the hen of the woods in layers tiered from trees, the extreme wildness of the speciation of these mushrooms all protruding from giant subterranean mats of mycelia in this eastern forest by a fallen forgotten quarry now just boulders, from which, in a different age, Irish stonecutters, beau's distant brethren, drove oxcarts hauling granite to build a college's chapel.

Here you walk the silence of the woods, rain softening the highest branches, shining leaves and bark. On return, cheerful in awe, you see the family's chickens, the rooster who greets you at first with his odd descending Dorian call, but then saddens you with his return to action: the rooster is pecking away at the inside of a misbegotten eggshell.

Atopos

Do you learn most
about love through
absence?

My father traveled with the zeal of someone believing he was doing the right thing for the world. Kenya, Honduras, Tanzania, Nicaragua, Guatemala. Anywhere the boils inside the earth argued against the surface, like a reverse fireman he showed up, ready to bring out its fire, and so, as he believed, help those who walked its surface. Renewably. Amid fumes of sulfur.

Stay warm or cool, cook, turn on lights by which to read, but geothermal development can now seem the fantasia of a bookish idealist who believes the interior redeems and is endlessly renewable. Once, he sent a beautiful tufted bird to me, its wings the color of fire, something I received in a sad home before I was five, on a postcard all the way from Africa, and I stroked it, imagining him inside a faraway continent. This was to love in absence.

While he sought to be useful to the earth, the three of us ate eggs. Eggs for every meal, as cooked by an arbitrary friend who descended, Obi from the kibbutz. For a long time, every egg tasted horribly of absence: left with Obi and my brother and Uncle Rick roosting with us.

In every picture from
that period, I look
down and away.
If I am smiling,
it is to myself.
If I am looking
at the camera,
it is with distress,
modified into a sort

of half-lidded curiosity
for school pictures.

Roland would say the mechanical analogue, the *denotation* of a myth—the participating schoolchild—binds with a *connotation* of despair, an alien, second-order message, ungraspable, and that *the photographic paradox can then be seen as the coexistence of these two messages.* That essentially one must invent a code to make or read any photo purporting to express reality, seeing in such official representations that the urge to make something *neutral* or *objective* makes anyone—school photographer, fellow kids, me—aim to copy reality meticulously, ending in something impossible, simultaneously a high-wire act: both ostensibly *natural* and *cultural*, in this case, the dance of the partly mothered child claiming to fit in. The wise wallflower pretending to smile at all the codes. My half-lids to my adult self stay my own private *punctum*.

We cannot read a photo without living inside codes: it is as if we try to make our way through a giant hall, from one end to the other, toward one window, one sluice of light, but the hall itself is strung through with geometric wire, taut, as if in a child's schoolyard game of cat's cradle: we bend and duck in and around the wire because these codes rule our perception and action, while we cannot quite see the wholeness of the light shimmering down from the window, we see it sliced by the tensility of codes, the wirelines. What lives is light, the mechanical analogue, a myth we hold about the meaning and height of the window. We dimly understand such myth. And at the same time as you make your way through the great hall of yarn, you invent your own code to survive and get to the other side, your own ball of wire tight in your fist buried in your pocket.

In nursery school, to soothe my lack of parenthood in the presence of bullies, I often went to sleep with a wad of chewing gum in my mouth and once woke with a pink network all over my face, a (predictive)(past) (impossible) replica of iodine poured as punishment on mother's legs as a child (of her, she in me, unnursed, we both sought comfort wherever it could be found). Solo toward the public, I embarked on the bus, my forever friends the window water beads and their hydrophilic dance of friction. And made the first mistake, believing stories could hide you. Lied to teachers, saying we had a cat and that the gum I slept with (that had ended up all over my face) was a kitten's scratch. Bad in the lie, hiding what I believed was my badness. (And so ended up skidding into my first failed fiction.)

When approaching a new anniversary with someone who had taught me what trust could feel like, I lived a continent away from him. A new sensation: to wake and believe in the faraway beloved. Rise into idealism and the day can dissipate it. Go downstairs and your nonvegan habits emerge: he is far away, harming nothing. You are here in your parsonage home, craving eggs. Trick to making eggs near a vegan: make them quickly, make no smoke (of ritual sacrifice), as if brevity mitigates the guilt. What the vegan knows: the consumption of embodied ideals capable of changing the world.

When one daughter entered my body, I craved meat suddenly, and she ended up a true carnivore, at least for some period of her life. While wherever he goes—people and their feasts, burning carcasses—scent accosts him; no matter the weather, he must go outside to breathe.

When we first got together, in the temporary post-nest, pre-parsonage apartment with its high ceilings and leaky porch, I hid and ate a boiled egg, an uncomfortable borrowing from days of an eating disorder, when my parents' different ways fought in my veins—the famished passion of my mother, the Germanic rectitude of my father—that era when death seemed preferable to continued struggle with the body-mind dialectic. So easy to replicate early solitude, to have it become the nomad's knapsack you take with you wherever you go. So easy to hide in the lost world in which an egg was all you would eat. Make a different choice, you can tell yourself, be the one who savors strawberries.

Imagine you cannot justify eating animals. Imagine the older boss who used to startle me, rubbing my arms sans consent, up and down, every time I saw him in our work site, all of us devoted to a Roland journal that also rose and died; he happened to be a famous meditator in our region and also something of a romantic hypocrite, the two traits not always untwinned. Once, he took me out to dinner with his far younger wife. *I honor the spirit of the animal when I eat it,* he said, *as the Tibetans do,* chewing the gristle.

Let us imagine your health seems to improve whenever you stray from being vegetarian—at what cost a fellow animal's life? Do you deserve to displace another? Imagine you drive older daughter to a gathering of people determined to survive apocalypse by learning to create their own tools. She will camp, and at some point in the weekend, a sheep will be slaughtered. Rams cause distress, they say, and your hypocrisy might also rear its head: how can they all hunker down nearby and watch the slaughter of an animal?

Consider what the newspapers report: abroad, as some slaughterhouse workers have gotten the glittervirus, 22,000 animals are being suffocated with horrid foam. *That's like what they did to the jews,* one daughter says, ripping open the ancient fridge, *Zyklon B.*

You and vegan beau drive to the walk a friend—a colleague—told you about, a saving grace in her teetering marriage. On a rail trail, you had run into her and she was surprisingly open. This era turns people into tins: some pried open, others wiring themselves shut, Anne Frank in the attic making not a peep.

At the head of the trail, a sign proclaims this state forest to remain open to hunters at all times.

When I was stationed down in a small southern town to help X with a project, a stranger, a kind lawyer and hunter, no oxymoron down south, saw fit to give me his broad-desked office to finish an article on Roland.

Just outright gave it to me, a stranger in town for a couple of months, his contradictions ordained by the Bible's true Author-God, as he saw it: *I have dominion over the fields* and also that other line of yarn *I must be kind to the stranger.* By some grace he let a jew-stranger pass with privilege into a holy site, his office. What kind of animal is she who feels forever hunted, belonging nowhere on this earth yet seeking to string together moments that matter as if temporal beads can make a place?

We walk in the woods and the carnivore talks with the vegan. The vegan startles, running after the dog across a meadow, shouting, to keep her from hurting a chipmunk, coming to soothe the dog from his upset by rubbing her belly. After a stunned moment, the chipmunk hops away. The carnivore says: *better the dog kill it now than that it be maimed.* A moment of silence under the trees absorbs this idea about predator and prey, but the argument cannot be swallowed.

More egg

Maybe useful here to consider the following about Roland: using the military jargon of the sanatorium, occasionally he would go on leaves to visit his mother. Each visit home reminded him how much she had to struggle to keep roof overhead, table laden with eggs and oranges every month. These jaunts tired him out; the house of mother was no sanatorium. Yet in the sanatorium, when sick, he had to reckon with long spells of enforced leisure, lacking music, company, writing, forced to be prone. Some of his most ardent readers turn to him to understand what happens in a bed, yet his words as arrows sought the zone of elsewhere, finding pleasure in targets foreign to the quiver, bed being both his prison and also the imagined place of unreachable meaning and pleasure; he could never write lying down.

His only distraction in bed back at the sanatorium: reading. And when he felt better, able to move about, able to sit and write, the place offered the pressure of mortality: how much he, like many, loved to write toward a deadline (he confesses as if to me this moment). He felt himself equivalent to young Julien Sorel in *The Red and the Black*, making bets against himself, on a final tour of Switzerland to ask material favors of wealthy Swiss.

I have always wanted to argue with my own moods (Roland writes, moodily).

So many grievances with himself, the text of his being polyphonic and feisty: he loves the music of Chopin but argues that he hates it, as only virtuosos can play his music. (Bourgeois socialist, he wishes for an art all can reach.) Some of his friends lack a clue about his sexual preference, which he aims to keep a casual unannounced trait, not wholly closeted. It is the attempt at casualness which ultimately betrays; the wife of one ostensibly straight friend visits another wife of another ostensibly straight man and whispers about Roland (syntagmatic stereotype, the predator), making that wife fear for her poor husband.

A scholar ruled by passion, Roland aims to evangelize others into loving the lineage of those who have influenced him, an elitist claiming royal kinship and then offering it to the masses. (He loves those who ignore others' boundaries.) His mother ignores his, forcing food on him as if he were a child (two hard-boiled eggs at eight every morning). He struggles with the betrayal of his body (wishing himself slim). After dinner parties, friends remark how he gobbles in an elemental, animal-like fashion. (One friend says he is like a lizard with a darting tongue.) Cold-blooded, sun-warmed, poikilotherm: alive, yet illness dogs him; some part of his rib is removed; he throws it away, wishing to be set free of it as if Adam throwing away the heterosexist binary, the mother-of-pearl inheritance.

To see the scraps of the world as part of a system of signs, a greater mystical mythology—his gift to us. Note the higher order in all that assails our days and choices and become then an informed consumer of signs: Roland believes in your ability to discern. Many have seen it, how much he still lives in our continued conversation, how we cannot tell where he begins and ends, given what cracked out of him.

Truth

Later how will we know this time? Will we call it the period when noise was sucked out of the universe as we joined together to heed the signal of existential dread and the requirement for celebration?

We celebrated eldest daughter's eighteenth birthday like royal roustabouts, defying fear of the glittervirus: a visit to a huge hot tub of the east coast styled as if it floated somewhere between Japan and California. On return, we picked up a silver tray of sesame balls for her to share with a nighttime trio of friends awkward near the tiny park across from the police station. Offered her, each day for a week, small gifts: a loofah (self-care), a renewable battery charger (survival). Self-care and survival: the song of this time. With the promise that meaning will arrive once we figure out how we live this day.

Late in the second semester, she recorded a song finally for her previous semester and, when I heard it, the song resounded as if coding the bumps of my own marrow. Between liturgy and lullaby, as if we'd sung it together yet entirely hers. Amusingly, the angel-faced teacher who probably had his own lost dreams responded in a message, singing back the opening in his voice.

Why do we not sing to and at
each other? How much better
our communications would become.

For so many years I went to the news to see: will all be okay? Her password has to do with everything still being okay: my brood finds ways to keep its feathers smoothed.

And yet there lives this pile-on in my psyche, repeating bad patterns of the past. For instance: each week during this time, in the dismemberment of mother's house, I must talk by phone with two other people and one of the fifteen selves of Uncle Rick. One of them is truly kind-hearted, wise, and compassionate, one a beleaguered kindergarten teacher, one a manipulative charmfest, one an angry apologist, a self-righteous activist for the self, one a late-night comedian, one filled with cheerful infantilism, one a sentimental family loyalist, one again a performatively hurt unappreciated martyr, one a sobbing child, one a cold dictator, one a smarmy enlightened person, and they cycle with interesting periodicity. Fine: why should the cycling of these selves trigger me?

The sassy shaman leads a ritual in which she asks me to imagine myself strong with secret unnamable allies. All I see: a sweet-faced owl peering down from a giant sequoia bearing a small female goddess head at its top, all the stature which I would soon need.

Disreality

Can you, despite interruption,
reenter the syntagm,
get back to that nighttime
car with me? What I did
right, according to
eldest daughter's aria—symbol and paradigm:

I drove her places. Listened.
Tried to provide.
I did not punish or criticize
for foolish things.

Like what?
(I asked, like my mother saying *why?*
after a compliment,
which really meant *say more.*)
Choice of friends, haircuts, habits;
allegedly, I showed up.
Did not neglect, the shadow
-fear of the writer-mother.
Do I take this in? No.

Because I rehearse dread: because my dispersed people trained my brain to skitter toward worry, from Yohanan the Sandalmaker in second-century Palestine all the way up through north Africa and western, eastern, central, northern Europe, the ancestral Maharal of Prague, Rashi, Baal Shem Tov, that odd line of Biblical commentators, shipworkers, salt-miners. The worriers fled and survived to send me their genes; those who stayed were killed. The earliest, made ghosts, never learned what let the later ones survive.

The inner message therefore becomes to question the text of orthodoxy, comment deeply and then find a way to flee magically: therein you find safety.

In these tendencies, of course a person could find kinship with semi-closeted Roland, who stayed cut off from wealthy grandmother's family, sympathetic to mother's plight, forever writing around Henrietta's presence and sense of lack, so that she ends up one of the world's most celebrated partially mothered daughters, a tribe for which I feel great affection. We readers attach unevenly to our authors for all sorts of reasons, just as a writer, Author-God or not, does in creating characters, and why would anyone wish to reduce the vastness of how a book is understood to the life that has been lived by its author? Roland's work is so much greater than his background; this, among all his points, is one he cared about most. He prefers the love resting in how a reader's understanding joins with that of their authors. And yet writers always twirl the spincraft of revelation, because they can't help themselves. Gustave Flaubert, oddly mothered, fellow traveler but semi-closeted man also liking rough trade abroad, on the huge nonmaternal projection he invented: *Madame Bovary, c'est moi.*

The Roland of these pages stays semi-fictive, as I feel this morning on the island's coast along which a hawk knows clear direction, flying over a cemetery of stone. My fingers turn an opaline blue like my father's on the steering wheel, driving away from my mother's tempest of feeling. Prone to Raynaud's syndrome, as JFK and he had, as I am, my fingers sting, hoping to spin something of worth to you.

First heart of the matter

Those people in your past, you never pined for anyone, eldest daughter says in front of newish love as we drive home from the field. *In high school or later. You never projected madly on any distant anyone, made up stories for months, you never had those people, you just ended up with people and tried to satiate your thirst for knowledge, adventure, travel.* A moment of silence; we both eye newish love. I stutter: what about the platonic girlfriend I had before college? Warm concordance floods the car. Eldest daughter agrees: *yes, the way you talk of your time of her. You are biromantic!* says new love.

Some months before, a first beau sits in a borrowed room in a friend's house across the country and with bare bulb behind him speaks of the phantom relation we have been having, apparently, since I was sixteen and he twenty-six, when at my behest my parents let him live in the home dismembered this year. Now I am more than twice the age he was at the time we started and yet those early heart compartments to which he introduced me bear his signature—silence, adventure, and intimacy mated within a couple. The fact of the ocean. The face of someone basking. The fate of dreaming with a being nearby.

Flattered and honored to hold such a place in his realm. Until the oddest moment, the ripcord encouraging brute honesty:

Well, R.D., what do you feel toward me?
I've always had love for you.
No. Say it. Say: I love you!

He reminded me of an unfortunate story: that he had asked me to marry him on a street soon after I had graduated college but I didn't fully remember until the moment came back *I thought you were joking* to which he said *I asked you lightly to protect myself, but we'd been together and it is customary—people marry—you were a person graduating from college—I asked—*

And he continued (my past self so skilled at presenting reasons for present self to ridicule it) *you said, Lots of people have asked me.*

I did? (Horrified.) *That's so heartless. I think I had the model of a male artist—that I had to go out and be in the world.*

He has given up being a film director, having owned a small diner at the edge of a ski resort. At sixty-three, he is applying to grad school in anthropology. Once he had been more connected to others, in a fraternity, with friends; an entire existence can pass. *I'm different,* he says.

I encounter millions of bodies in my life; of these millions, I may desire some hundreds; but of these hundreds, I love only one, Roland says. If he is on some spectrum, so am I, the term spectrum disorder not so common when long-ago beau and I commenced. Perhaps together we created my lifelong romantic spectrum. Sharing experience and thinking deeply inside, I believed, was that not enough?

Roland confesses: *I thought I was suffering from not being loved, and yet it is because I thought I was loved that I was suffering; I lived in the complication of supposing myself simultaneously loved and abandoned.*

Catastrophe

A mother dies and everyone is aflame with advice. The way the heirs should take care of the physical assets should become a child's game. *Take turns!* One person, then another, colored dots with chemical glue you can—just like that!—affix to sentiment: each person claims something. *The greater value rests in the memory. The things do not carry memory. Just let go.* The people who say this do not lack for material goods. And yet do you really want your life to be about this project management? Especially when it's not a tight relation.

Do you think your non-uncle Rick will end up homeless? It is not impossible. He had ended up suing others or being sued, the story kept twisting its codes, biting its own tail, so that he ended up back in your mother's house, awaiting the last suitors to pay him off but somehow he ended up near-destitute, claiming his stay was for her own good. An unfunny uncle, present at all the wrong times. As with anyone, he had his benign sides, that damp cloth he lay on your fevered forehead, the old-fashioned red hot-water bottle for your belly, the insistence on wiping a mirror down, but after the death of your mother, as with your divorce and X, many come up to you to say that Rick is mentally ill. So smart he seems, you cannot quite believe it.

How great is Rick's metacognition about everyone else, prone to citing platitudes: you almost cannot believe that a man so clever in mustache and trenchcoat, hiding in habits of an Italian opera aficionado, his chess-playing café now virtual, could be off-kilter; now he spends most of his time a bit stunted, beating teens in Kiev or Taiwan.

What is mental illness? (*Ah,* someone says, *the 64,000-dollar question.*)

Who decided on 64? (*Ask R.D. Laing.*)

Who, at heart, is R.D. Laing? (The one who said there is no mental illness and freed so many back in the sixties.)

In so many details, Rick cannot manage life. *What does this mean,* you ask. Rick drives a car stuffed with a hoarder's paradise of stuff (you have had this attribute). He spends a great deal, coming to parties laden with a potlatch of generosity. (You have done this at times.) His virtual chess, his trenchcoat, his golf vacations, all that puts him into debt, the beach-side timeshare condos on stilts over climate change. (You share with him the search for love.) He has two grown and alienated ex-stepsons but still subscribes to parenthood magazines. (You have also tried to learn to be a parent.) Fun times with a toddler! Articles on making memories with kids!

Times when Uncle Rick most wanted to manipulate your mother, he used an odd infantile voice: he would make it go up a half-octave and slow down, as if he forever patronized his little friend and he were a knowing child circa age twelve.

Advice surrounds you.

Can your head see out
of this thicket?

Burn it all down.

Even before her dying days when the frequency increased, your mother would confess to you and her caregivers that she felt manipulated by Rick and the voice he used. That he kept vanishing, never around when she needed him. Yet she could never say no to him, he always had to be right, he used his words too well. Finally, she wrote him in as executor. The second she passed, he began the myth of how his days were filled with his caring for her.

You visited him once before he moved in with your dying mother, his tiny pre-flood apartment filled with flyers from weekend retreats regarding how to find romantic partners and superior ketogenic diets. His freezer had been filled with neatly compartmentalized freeze-dried foods as if these alone could help him manage life.

Why bother being in touch with him, certain friends kept asking. These friends happen to have been born with that silver spoon of self-sovereignty, the ability to play that bartender with the stentorian straightforward voice after last call, a role far beyond your capacity. Despite your ripe age, how hard to make boundaries. The most severely cut prisms cast the most glorious rainbow hues. What does it mean to cut someone off? If today were your last day of life, in which color do you most wish to believe? The forgiving bending hue that admits no past angle or the sharp light in which those of your past become dark forms, cut-out silhouettes, the litotes of this text, with all its holes expanding to swallow even where this life sentence should end.

Palimpsest

First given me by a friend, the mattress in the bedroom.

In this time, everyone and their relationships spiral like smoke. The women especially seem to be rumbling the ground, restless. One bit of research reports that the only documented difference in the assigned-female brain is the thicker corpus callosum, a neural link between hemispheres: according to this study, a female stroke victim might regain language more quickly, as if more prone to multitasking, berry-picking rather than the hunt, shopping for multiple items: my gender-nonconforming beau questions the test's very parameters. And yet may it be said that during our collective stroke, this float, those identifying as women (birth, behavior, identity) seem to hunger for new berries. One local woman who happens to share my name, a kerchiefed trans dancer who once sat next to me in a group, ends up unable to survive the isolation: R.D., may her memory survive as a blessing.

As crocuses start nudging umber leaves, my dead mother hurts more. Husks fall away, mourning revives. The possibility starts to feel real, that I could return to her marital bedroom where, in solitary waning, she slept with dim lights, forever ready for horsemen who might come a-knocking. Athwart the wall, the driftwood antler holding dusted love, travel necklaces from my wayward father above so many other signs and gifts, ancient squeezable perfume bottles, a pearl I once inhaled dangerously into a nostril so as to breathe in her absence. Thick swirled mugs, bright patterned scarves. Why did I not understand? Death clarifies the tardy insight: love of the lavish let her navigate the body-mind divide. Through objects, she sought to share the bounty of joy with others, her hugs, dance, and scarves of the same cloth. Not just prudent materialism borne of the Depression, but an embrace of human-made hues. Redwoods and ocean's tangy air thrilled her, but especially lovable: humans who alchemized bliss from the bad, the ecstasy of human creation. The mad ones, the talkative ones. Art! The very fact of it startled her awake.

On visits, I tiptoed into her room. Her baseline waking state: a startled girlishness. *O hello!* She wanted to be awake, ready, eternally a student. A woman who wished to be alive, who would stir no matter what. And then who asked for massage. Her spine with the S of scoliosis especially loved the one western skill my hands held—not homesteading, gold-panning, nor macramé: massage.

Once, an eastern friend whom I met in a filmmaking class in Manhattan looked at my family photo of a bellydance party and found her particular punctum, saying: *I can't imagine this:* a tumble of people in full puppy pile off an embroidered couch, the western body-friendliness as foreign as was her family's Manhattan to me, that blindingly white apartment overlooking the high East River in which a low untouched bookcase hosted a heavy array of ornamental black iron knives: impeccable a priori hygiene, singular cultural imprint, ostensibly neutral, inviting certain proclivities. The hand's end: knives being a history-swallowing technology amid the heavy symbolism of money.

Out west, you learn to use your hands toward amnesia: massage to take away the difficulties of the past, the opposite of an epitaph. At a party in northern California as a child, you find massage a form of saying hello. People don't drink, they put their hands on another's shoulders, feet, hands, their thumbs grinding away all history held by connective tissue. Only in esoteric circles on the East Coast, say, in the dance world of contact improvisation world which I briefly visited at the end of my marriage, did I see the same culture: this need to announce (by touch not speech) this bare fact of being mammals together.

Just as our puppy keeps asking for anyone's body nearby.

And so one daughter shines this bright face at me this morning, having woken, having temporarily replaced my beau in the morning bed, she soon to go off, to college or not, her smile still as if she were an infant, that same brightness, and yet she says she has been sub-depressive this year, this lack of movement that has beset us all, meditating on home, she asks me to massage her skull, a way of saying hello and goodbye, swallowing the bad.

Inexorably
spring is making me
long to massage my mother.

And in this season, as we all were attempting new forms of health, I tried for one week a little white pill meant to keep that long-dormant autoimmune issue, unrelated to our collective float, from worsening. For years, I had known no greater impediment than cold hands and occasional insomnia; lab numbers reported worse. Still, the little pill, even in its lowest dose, designed for those coming off heroin addiction, blocked opioid receptors. And so, as in the darkest days of the marriage, I lost at the same time two hands: my wish to write and the capacity for joy. One week into the white pill, I had to stop. Was the double helix at my core an anxious opioid-starved wish to reach out and connect through words? What's the point of it all, I wondered. Not serious ideation, just the untouchable shades of the past: the flitting that had awaited me down dark streets

should the leaves be raked
should the word be writ
should I stop to savor
can I savor
should I stop

Compassion

I had three beings depending on me and suddenly had ten. I stand and nod listening to another man talk about the physical universe to me. You must grade the land if you want to put in your writer's shed. You must have someone come and take out all the dead trees. At noon, your friend wants you to do a daily meditation with her: breathe in the black pain of others and breathe out light. Right now your throat is scratchy, your land ungraded, your Institute restitution manual unread, your own book unwrit, and to breathe in suffering goes against the tiredness of six A.M.

To understand

The dream was of going to the megahealth grocery and a moment comes in which blackout curtainflaps are pulled down:

The store employees have
become police. The one checking

the sanitation has everyone line
up, arms outstretched. You don't

want to touch someone but now
we are asked to do so. Disobediently,

I see as if in a line dance I can
circle the line toward the entrance.

Why don't we just leave?
Why don't we just go to the parking lot?

The anxiety is so great, the dream is
its reward. Apologies to Milton, it is better to line

up and obey than flee.

Behavior

That somebody starts to judge more. That another starts to feel vulnerable to judgment, as the openness of branches to wind becomes more solitary, lacking human gaze. On the secret paths threaded along the college town's rivers, the mix of those who inhabit nature changes. The nature now belongs to everyone and each brings habits of the city to the brink. For eons, humans knew the wisdom of the riverbanks which had no need for the wisdom of humans about any eon. And now trucks haul the provender of rivers to the mouths of those who forgot how to say thanks.

The text from the friend's husband is curt: *we want to talk to you about social distancing.* The friends don't want my beau to be around their son, my daughter's friend. These are not bourgeois mores. This is old love rejecting the new.

Connivance

The dreams of that time
drag you through your past with
a willy-nilly intensity.

Your dead mother speaks with her
sister who ate herself to death.

Because you are messy, a man
thinks he can follow you into
corners abandoned by the populace.

A hotel with no one staying in it.

Such has been the state of
your joy. You start a journal
which you began two years
earlier, and though you live
tenuously, the hammock of your
life conspires to swing in one
direction: gratitude.

Body

In the cold outside the body inside
is hungry for that which it cannot
have. And yet in the middle of
the night the body next to you is so
beautiful you make love to the idea
of beauty itself without waking
anyone or touching anything but
the way the air rests upon the side
of your cheek, gazing upon him.

Contingencies

If you tell the former mate that the current mate is now in the home, does the anger mess up everyone's immune system? Do you wish to have your children live with untruth? *Don't tell him,* they say, *he will be angry.* Marriage exploded, you left and no longer must tiptoe around the anger. He is a good person. Yet he has a shard of himself that only you have seen, you and his dead dad, and it is a scary rage. The kids have seen most of it; you have seen it all.

But what is the right thing to do? Others have said: *you are not cohabiting, this is unprecedented quarantine.* But in the unprecedented, don't we still get to have truth? The kids are not adults. You want to tell the former mate. Is it better to tell him when the kids are heading for their week in his house, your old home, or will they then bear the brunt of his anger? So much of your family system was constructed around fear of anger, not just his.

Your youngest child says, astutely, *you want us to be the adult pacifier?* You get advice: tell Vegas mate about the new quarantined cohabiting beau when the kids are away from him so they do not have to bear the punch. *Who will write the history of tears?* Roland asks, and also at another point, of his mother's birthday *all I can offer her is a rosebud from the garden. At least it's the only one, and the first one since we're here.* We do whatever we can to offer anyone love, good timing sometimes its simplest coin. Is that enough?

Smitten

Some people create boundaries and
feel wonderful, declaring the self. Others
feel contemptible.

One of the reasons you asked for the divorce was you no longer wanted to be mad. People get angry at injustice: a system, a history. The grief hardens into grievance. You no longer wanted to be the mad mother or mate, and you wanted to leave the conversational games: who was at fault? Who was the biggest martyr or victim? Who was being a freier, as X's croupier pawnbroker father always told him not to be: a sucker, and in this schema, who played sucker, who suckee? Who did not get what? You did what you could.

But to find yourself mad and then your new beau in the middle of the night soothing you: you have imperfection. Yes. But then you can also be loved.

Roland here is of little help: *What do we call the subject who persists in an 'error' against and counter to everyone, as if he had before himself all eternity in which to be 'mistaken'? Whether it be from one lover to the next or within one and the same love, I keep 'falling back' into an interior doctrine which no one shares with me.*

Will there be problems ahead: if new beau has future children, will he be underslept, will you both get mad? (Memory of hiding with brother as father stormed in, angry at a poorly cleaned household: this informed your later pattern.) Will you ever feel upset about anything connected to new beau? Does anger have to be such a scary shadow thought? This becomes one part of what Roland would call the enigma code of our story.

I look for signs, but of what? What is the object of my reading? Is it: am I loved (am I loved no longer, am I still loved)? Is it my future that I am trying to read, deciphering in what is inscribed the announcement of what will happen to me, according to a method which combines paleography and manticism?

but also

In the encounter, I marvel that I have found someone who, by successive touches, each one successful, unfailing, completes the painting of my hallucination

and yet for that moment *I am totally given over to this discovery.*

Dependence

Mother buried
under burnt dirtclods
in the unchanging
season that is northern California.
Despite what people say, grief
claims all seasons and none
yet you, if jew, are meant to mourn
for eleven months.

You'll feel it,
the Californian mystics claim,
she'll be nearby: forty days and nights,
three months, six months.
You will see treetops, birds, flickered
electricity, balls of energy in corners:
all will signify mother.

And you will see, after a year you'll feel
her, she will come to you, saying goodbye.

The mystics of California love to be all-knowing; knowledge is seductive; hence mystics are seductive.

Pascal made a famous wager: given the grand prize, might as well believe in God. During your lifetime, act as if God exists, and you sacrifice certain worldly pleasures, the penalty finite. Yet should God turn out to exist, get the infinite reward and go home free!

Roland complains from Morocco, *seeing the swallows flying through the summer evening air, I tell myself, thinking painfully of* Maman*: how barbarous not to believe in souls—in the immortality of souls!* cursing himself: *the idiotic truth of materialism!*

Declaration

One of the most painful parts of writing is revealing oneself. This should be obvious, but it is not. When I was young, Uncle Rick consistently read my diary. *I can't help it,* Rick said, *your writing is so good.* And there was the rub. The first reader to like your work had already violated internal space in more than a few ways: would you wish to share or hide?

Later there was a first writing teacher, his eyepatch making him a swaggering pirate of literature, and how with his writer friends—what a glorious concept to the impressionable mind—they spoke more of the biz of writing, agents and the like, rather than the act itself. His grand injunction was one Roland might have loved: *write what you don't know!* Another mentor traveled the world, work soaring upon research, a habit against which he warned. Long had he wanted to be recognized as a fiction writer and yet how well he modeled the life of constant escape and flight.

How might you mix such influences? Say you were working as a waitress in a garden restaurant off the boardwalk south of Santa Monica and a man often came in, a lawyer, and he always asked: *how does a young writer manage to write, work, research, and live life?* What could be the answer? At that age, curiosity topples over patience.

Say that instead in that period you moved three times over eighteen months and held no job longer than a month. And in this fable, soon one day there came some publication of your Roland work with a stray mention of a grandfather and a relative of yours was disturbed: *you dishonor memory, I am used to seeing you as magnanimous, please never write about me or my family.*

The revelation of the inner bad
self: this is what writing can do too.

For years, the worst thing you had done was read the journal pages of that older beau. After you confessed, he asked to see the journal you were keeping in your twenties and remarked: *it is amazing to see how you are so confident in your interior!* Here is the rub of writing; you observe (along grotto walls), the eye keeping its faith when the rest of you or the world might not. The possibility of getting to name sometimes erodes the very state it seeks to attain: the ecstasy of understanding!

Middle daughter, adolescent, walks the beach amid the family of revealed humanity, exclaiming: it is so wonderful, these people and the charisma of the ocean, I become nothing. *You lose your ego!* you find yourself saying, cheerful in naming too egoically her triumph.

Ode to the owl

We have gone for a masked bike ride, the friend and I, on one of the first sunny days. To a new swing where she enjoys herself with great girlish whoop. We see, from far below on the field, an older serious woman approach.

This friend says of an earlier mate that they are forever linked, having fellow cubbyholes in the universe next to each other, while some current mate and she stay only on swings, parallel, enjoying the temporary ride, soon to jump off. Who might you be with anyone?

The night before, I had been alone at the table; middle daughter had made an exquisite diorama, a tiny version of our lives, a tempest in a giant ark-like house, loving, witty, exact. Youngest daughter stormed upstairs, having stated yet again that it is hard to be quarantined with new mate; everyone fierce in passion, lions retired to their quarters. What will be the right course? I turned to one of my mother's last videos to me, when I knew we were having one of our last visits. Hooked up to oxygen, she speaks with verve and courage, emphasizing and inventing words, unhitched from language, any one of Roland's codes floating up to the great noosphere:

> *My wish for you is that* ***the motto for sake*** *becomes an absolute value in you! And you're able to adjust to what they're giving you. And get your* ***had*** *for everything that you put into this* ***amaryst****. And that they give you a consistent* ***paybill****. What you dearly deserve! And it becomes a* ***matrych*** *for you to* ***wrestle in****.*
>
> *And you get your deserved in* ***the rights of the demon****!*

Her passion lives: she wants her children to be met by the world. Though, whatever the rights of the demon, no bird could sight the pornography of screens in our time. In this case, let porn denote the *orchestrated series of gesture toward preconceived outcome.* Take all the lectures and literary readings in which people gesticulate or appear composed toward the camera of their own gaze. Our interactions in this time of pixels would have been so different had none been able to see themselves. While meanwhile the aleatory, flattening porn of screens will not stop, overtaking concepts of soul, serendipity, destiny.

Paranoia multiplies across these screens. *He doesn't love me, she thinks poorly of me, they are bad, I don't belong in the visual stream.* These calls we hear down the corridors of our empty burrows after—if ever—we turn everything off. *The real is not representable,* Roland would tell them.

I tell my friend how the students of our disbanded Roland Institute are crying, they are alone. One appears in the window square of the computer and says: *I never know who I am until I begin talking to another.* One tells me of the need to schedule true connection time with their mate, because otherwise the two barely put up with each other in their small apartment. Another keeps insisting there might be imminent departure to Brooklyn, that promised land, though the prior statement had concerned the wish to stick around while a mate finishes a degree. People are seeking escape.

The friend on the swing talks to me and then her eyes alight on a tree behind: *an owl,* she says, *I have a friend who taught me to look for owls, my eyes are always cast away from whatever is around us, or looking out for a threat, even a dog on the trail, but my friend can spot everything, people in love, mushrooms, owls. In a day we find it all.*

And as the older serious woman in the field walks uphill toward the swing, she reveals herself to be a girl who turns out to be eldest daughter with her head newly, shockingly shaven and our puppy. *You always find our father,* she says of Vegas mate, who with other daughters will soon, apparently, approach. The universe has its jokes: I never go to this swing, all those years I probably never quite found him, my heart gone seeking so that realness found me elsewhere. Perhaps, to use my mother's terms, I may not have got my had from the amaryst, but this was my own matrych in which to wrestle. And yet from the owl's view, everyone is always aligned, moving toward rightful ends upon the surface with little friction.

We talk: the owl flies out over the valley, its wings tremendous, and was it an owl after all, a hawk or, even more unlikely, an eagle? Can we believe what we see and feel and have it stay vast as the unnamed world or does story send it fleeing?

The idea

This morning I read what I had written of a dream my father had a few months before he died. He had been wild-eyed, his helper said, and needed to call me. On the phone, his voice was urgent: *are you planning on crossing to the other side,* he asked. *I really wondered if you'd gotten tickets—made arrangements. Are you asking if I was planning on committing suicide?* I asked. The stink of death can be removed so simply, once you near it. *Yes. No,* I said. But in truth the shade was near; in my marriage, I was burning out goodwill and telomeres besides.

This was some years after my new beau began his crush, though I did not know. Some years after I came close to wondering what it was all for. My father linked to me not just in this way but in his predilection for aqueous floating knowledge.

And then another old video today of my undead mother popped up on my phone, making a verbal legacy for all three of my daughters. Nouns shift, verbs stay mostly intact. This is the wisdom of the end of life: nouns don't matter. Spend most of our lives chasing them as we do, but in the end, as with fiction, verbs—and adverbs, and even the adjectives—matter most.

One of those most-quoted poems by my former mentor, Robert, his meditation at Lagunitas, has a few nouns uttered in italics. When I was young, they seemed invocations of pleasure. *Blackberry, blackberry.* Older, after so many shades visited me, the nouns seem icons of mortality. Is there a difference?

Demons

After her death, imagine this legacy: you have
learned how important it is to listen.

The old-time linguist says men (gendered as such) are taught to do report talk while women do rapport talk. *What are your concerns?* Uncle Rick says, in professional mode.

You tell him what you've heard: there are liquidators, a pair of loving sisters, they will comb through and rid the lost home of all mother's belongings. And that it is a good idea to apportion a long day or weekend, the heirs take turns, find a storage facility to store objects that take too much sentiment or thought to trawl: albums, journals. A place communally rented. Not unaware of hostility, you go too much into details, as if to padlock your history.

You have become the bad person. It is an upward struggle, this reach toward the golden ring of self-compassion, hard to grab from your seat on the merry-go-round, a plastered owlchair, paint chipping. *The golden ring awaits you but you sit too low to reach it.* You must either destroy the merry-go-round or else merely (Roland loves puns a little too much) destory it.

Drama

The hypervigilant brain, trained over many centuries, has been selected for survival. And so you wake another morning having dreamt of being bullied by Uncle Rick, first perpetrator. And then go to pick up children from the house of Vegas mate where you lived your last light-bereft days, a home where other marriages had also gone up in flames. To pick up children: not an experience of ceaseless delight but rather an eon of sitting in a cold dark car, an hour and a half, two hours, some cruelty in the minute-hand, how these transitions continue.

Middle daughter appears, face stricken: *we just started a bonfire,* the act suggested by your Vegas mate, no stranger to conflagration, the fire starting long past the hour you were to pick them up.

I hate being a killjoy, you say, *this puts me in an awkward position.*

And the three girls in the car finally emerge, flippancy a flameproof shield. *Maybe our father should bring us next time?*

Yes, but you won't come (on time).

We never come on time for anyone anyway, one says, sinking your heart in prayer. Let them not inscribe themselves into living aslant communal agreement, let them be able to keep their own.

He can't drive us?

In the silence, a recall of Vegas mate. Soon after the marriage had exploded, soon after you declared the wish for the divorce, he spoke to you affably, speaking of his lower back and its issues. The problem of a leaky gutterpipe, an overhanging branch. He held the ladder for you tenderly, and you saw the way the divorce might unfurl, the two of you companionable on the road called life, moving forward, that twinkle-fingered new constellation of your sky. You wish for peace, does he not want the same? You mounted the ladder, he seemed to be holding tight and firm, until he ended up seized by a fit, the sneezing often used to announce his presence. So intense that he shook the ladder, hard, and then kept shaking, his hands entering a trance as was the case with certain policemen of this time,

he could
not let go
of the grip.

The way you experienced
the falling
in slow
motion, down and around, magically
rolling

as if you had planned this from a karate movie, down across your shoulder and around so that, though you were bruised, after a moment of shock on the ground, you could rise (as if from the marriage) intact.

You could walk away.

The kids saw this from behind the orange curtain of the upstairs window. As you limped back to your car to return to the new temporary other place, a cabin with a woodstove in which you felt the rush of restoration, your own energy surging as if for the first time, music with broad slowing cadence, he shouted at you, as was often the case if you hurt yourself: *what, you want to blame me for this?*

(And stretched out far behind his shout, as you can feel for his own case, some long legacy of shame made him hear blame everywhere.) It would have been almost fine but for the other incident: the package he mailed with strange dust puffing out that laid you low for a day. *What do you want, I couldn't help it,* he yelled over the phone, *you blame me for working with rat poison that day, who can be a hundred percent hygienic all the time, didn't mean to* voice tinniest right before hanging up.

Why did he have it in for you? Not bad at heart; of course everything could be explained away.

When you were aiming for new twinkle-family constellation, he for the first time suggested a trip, on inflatable kayaks, borrowed from a friend, a nearby pond. What amazing enterprise he showed; you didn't know he had it in him; perhaps this was the new functional hidden by years of marriage. You were cheered, you entered a version of (father's)(later beau's) picturesque. The happy post-divorce family! He would make plans, all would thrive. You helped each of the three girls go off on their boats and then stepped into the boat designated yours: an unseaworthy vessel. Later you saw all the places the plastic had been stabbed, meant to spring leaks. He and the three kids had their outing; you watched from shore until you could watch no more.

And the last and worst incident. (Let it be forgotten.)

O yeah, daughter says, *I forgot.*

And say the next day you wake feeling unworthy and terrible, that symbol and syntagm: *the bad mother*. Bad in all ways: bad keeper of equanimity, money, house, secrets, bad burnisher of the symbolic order of the realm.

You take the dog on a walk since no one else wants to and what is there to write on Roland anyway? Your pockets weighted, heavy with logistics and bureaucracy.

On the phone, a friend tells you her woes: a rain of intrusive thoughts. This is what happens when we receive uneven parenting: intrusive thoughts enter as substitute for pelt, cave, fire.

At home you get an email called *pet the lizard*, about how we many times in the day must find a way to soothe our reptilian brain, reminding the lizard that it can emerge from its rock with no concern about time.

In this case, your beloved meets the lizard. Readying himself for a shopping expedition, to stand in the sun with others holding phones, masked. Except in this case he wears over his head the scarf your mother gave you, green swirled flamboyance, and the buccaneer costume oddly reminds you of the earliest tender and gleefully *invited* face he wore when you met him all those years ago.

He is also heading out to deposit a check for you. Could you be more grateful? *You look like a ship's boy,* you say: he loves this and basks. That the choice of serving another has become part of your dreamlife: is this not the ultimate luxury?

You will die a happy person if you can play on the instrument of yourself the score of your to-do list without drama. Aspire from the innermost center; the lizard wants no more. No one will fall, get sick, burn, explode. Your X is doing okay, telling you that after the divorce his health improved. All dramas rise and fall, and what will make it out of this story fully alive? Freedom, connection, or the unchartable in-between?

Flayed

11:11, 12:12, 1:01, deep into the new morning, the girls giggling.

You go in and three sisters are getting along.

Not always a common occurrence, but everyone in the house, beau, tenant, you, all have been awakened by their hijinks. It would be one thing if they heard what you said and then immediately went to sleep. But instead high spirits continue, puppy in the mix, who does not sleep crate-trained (the dream of order) but on the ground next to daughter #2 in her preferred mode, mattress on the floor, window open. Liking the savage, a child of nature. To eat from a pan with two hands, filled with gusto. Part of the whirl of their being is a warm joyful wit, but their loudness and hexagonal gaze can feel like impudence.

The gentle heart of Roland with his mother in the morning, tapping teaspoons in steady rhythm against soft-boiled eggs in heirloom cups, hoisted as the last of riches pried from stern ungiving grandmother's house, son and mother making gentle wry jokes before silence—such stillness is not your home.

Some forms of anger come from a rightful sense of injustice, a friend keeps saying. But how amazing, now permanently awakened, 1:30 am, in the kitchen with your beau showing up to hug you. *I feel what you feel,* he says. He wants to help the kids and also wishes to hold your back: have you ever known this before?

A friend writes the next morning that she told her children to find a puppy born the day she dies and she will come back as that puppy to be loved and stand by them (as you wish to stand by yours).

Some say anger roots itself in earliest misunderstood beliefs: entitlement, insult, a form of neurotic attachment. Adults make agreements but children have one-sided expectations: anger dents the bridge toward maturity.

There are some people with whom you must be transactional and others with whom you are relational, counsels a friend. You had long thought the key to survival had always been to keep your heart open, limitless.

There live those who understand fences, marking the ego's limitations and needs, or those who say the secret code is to keep oneself open to love, soft and trusting, to proceed with compassion always, even with aggressors, even with Vegas mate, to never take a stand. Your recipe: you had turned aggressors into your own private Stockholm Syndrome party: you could see why they were aggressive even as you flew out of your body. What right did you have to mark the terrain of your body, to take a stand?

To write

Roland believes reading is a form of writing and that writing brings you into being. At a low point in the relation, you had forgotten who you were, so you made a child's list of items you liked, as you had forgotten. You had become so dedicated to telos, the far-off goal, you had turned into a robot of survival. You went to work, you met people's concerns, you scraped the lowest part of yourself out and served it to the masses. As if to say: see this gruel! It had been some years since you felt.

Imagine feeling yourself an alien living among others. Might you one day be inducted into the tribe of those who know what they want? On arrival at the eastern college, I was shocked to find these hardened girls of the isle of Manhattoes or other cultural archipelagoes who opined with their hard noses and jut jaws of needs, wishes, and interpretations in a way that requested no lateral reading: was this the way to be? To know with definitives, to profess knowledge of all ends?

While to avoid stating anything with certainty allowed for a certain western perfectability, my father's aqueous soul, the possibility of movement as in metaphor which lifts meaning from one realm and transposes it elsewhere. Can we enjoy the journey? Is that such a hard goal?

And yet can you state a need, from the self, and stay in a relationship? Can you be loving, unattached to outcome, and still speak some truth in a shared journey? Some people have finessed this skill. Might you at a late age get to enter that most special alien tribe?

The cuttlefish and its ink

It is so hard to give up this urge to be seen. How does one finally see oneself enough?

We always will meet difficult people, the genius friend says. The antidote vision: picture yourself with roots going through damp earth and underground rivers and bedrock to the fiery core, then shooting up into a giant tree overhead, the bigger picture. You get to have a boundary around yourself.

But what happens when you identify with captors too young and so lack a self, and read too much ego-burning buddhism at too formative an age?

What hope for you if early on you wished to banish ego, becoming transparent as a form of survival? Imagine that later you must do all mind-tricks to establish an ego: a purplish aura egg of protection. These roots the friend suggests. That you too can enter humanity, you too get to speak the truth from your heart. How wonderful that might be.

Do others stay rooted in the face of difficult people? As if a child, I want the difficult people to be happy.

We crave certain forms of elaboration to help us find ourselves in the specific. Nabokov used to give a final exam at Cornell with only one question: what is the color of the wallpaper in Anna Karenina's bedroom? It is the details and how we savor, relinquish, or manage them that makes us great as the sky.

I was living a bit
blindered, in a picket
-fence hell of my own
making, and I had
forgotten myself.

So I tried, as in *Harold and the Purple Crayon*, the great children's story in which Harold summons up all that is lacking in his environs—a ladder into the stars—to write, yet I had this idea of discipline, of daily word quotas as a way to cheat the superego and find a backdoor key into the garden of wonders. The problem was that the cheating of the superego became, in its own way, the superego.

And so I had to recall a list of things I liked, because I had become such a creature of servitude—children and art and work—that I forgot the core:

cardamom
making fairy castles out of twigs and moss by the river with the youngest

It is oddly these small pleasures that can remind us of who we are. Do you know what it means to put a pinch of clove in your coffee and be reminded of a narrow cobblestoned alley in Andalucía and the fatalism of that sad man in the tetería who felt his life had only ceiling, and you first rubbed against your Californian birthright horizon-banishing apart from your family's travails, an endless can-do optimism, that gift of the first part of your life?

Most art rises from fascination and its attenuation—you must be divorced from a thing to know that it could be of interest. Hemingway often said the following: that to write about a place you must be far from it. What if you are far from the self? And to which self do you write?

Embrace

Sometimes only music helps. The student says he came to the Roland Institute solely on the strength of whatever casual warmth happened to be the particular music of your mood that day.

Recall this: a small sink in the tiny room that was one of mother's studies in that rambling house that became an expression of her wish to study, each room an office, bought for nothing back when that part of Berkeley was considered troubled.

Her scientist mind appreciated the house did not sit on such a steep hill that one would have water issues. Atop the small office sink, a pile: one dried rose bouquet upon another, given her after past performances. She lacked the heart to throw even one out. Maybe thirty bouquets dried but drunk from the happiness of past evenings, a hoarder's monument rebuking what hung above: the colorized fearsome hanging photo of her mother the critic and a father too fearful and hard-working to protect.

What does it mean to
perform before another?

You may wish for their attention for a period: they see you, everyone feels seen, love flows. The imperfect time-swallowing tense of bouquets: chosen before seeing your work, open or lustrous buds proffered, attesting your performance was fresh and perfumed but that art blooms eternally. In the farmer's markets of Los Angeles you find fresh fruit and flowers, yes, but also a local rarity: preserved roses that never age. People still hungering for love, well-hatted beneath the punishing sun, poke at these bouquets: immortal yet lifelike!

Say you store that bouquet. If you were born near the Depression, you always know the risk of scarcity. Hold on and store because there will never be enough bouquets, and at your death, you will wish to plunge into the most delicate velvet-tinged rose petals. Could there ever be enough love?

Regretted

I feel she stays here
with me yet keeps right on
changing. We know death
to be asymmetrical but right now this
writing might call her here.

Mourning: a cruel
country where I am no longer
afraid (Roland says
after the burial of Henrietta).
Yet also: *henceforth*
and forever,
I am my own mother.
His dear mother's slights
informed his,
her unlived life his piston.

Habiliment

Your daughter happens to be wearing a shirt. Black, neck angular, collar jeweled. A mother's eyes finds it astonishingly beautiful.

Where did that come from? Did I get that for you, as you usually ask. (The two questions also apply to nature and nurture: the basic surprise being that someone is linked to you without being exactly like you. Compañeros del camino, soulmates, fellow sojourners.)

Remember? The used-clothes store?

(So many sites pass before you: dustlight scalding angles on leftover hopes.)

Can you remember which side of the border, she asks, eyes bearing a riddle. *Greek or Turkish?*

The one we went to with S?

Your sooty memory: S yet another hyper-competent mother in the league of those you have collected. Neighborly, altruistic, opinionated, one of many who have triangulated affections with your daughters. This daughter she told to buy a sackdress, that daughter's own mother didn't know how lovely shone the young knees that should be shown.

Stunned mute and accepting, Stockholm syndrome, you listened to louder bleats. So often you felt the entitlement of being someone's mother was barely yours: only gleanings should be yours, the dusty used clothes of others.

An echo in your imagination, during those early days of being a mother: the biblical Ruth. *Wherever you go,* Ruth says to her mother-in-law Naomi *I will go; wherever you rest, I will rest. Your people shall be my people, your god my god. Where you die, I will die—there I will be buried. This much and more, let this happen should anything but death separate me from you.*

Say you felt in your first acts as a mother as if like Ruth, ready to live in the foreign land of new forms of love, knowing mainly this brute deep inchoate loyalty toward these kids.

Early on, toward these little sheep, you felt you could learn mothering only by proxy. Shouldered next to other real parents in the sandlot or playgrounds, you could study. One day, like the velveteen rabbit, you might become real. Pick and choose: the consumer marketplace of contemporary parenthood. Who do you want to be? Believe yourself, like Ruth, forever a foreigner, immigrant to the land of mothering. Belong to the realm of mothers mainly by analogy. Be that eager student, an apprentice! Not a mother-in-law but a daughter aspirant and mother-in-name. (Only Winnicott helps, whispering it is enough to be *good enough.*) Not that you had to invent the wheel. The wheel exists. It is just a juggernaut which—with your ideals, your belief in perfectability—could run you into the ground.

There are certain parents whose ideals are so high, they can only sustain the performance of parenthood for a brief interval in the day and then are exhausted by the paces through which they put themselves. The smileyface organic perfect parent who then desperately dials the babysitter for a 40-hour stint the following week, or who must thrust the child down for more than a few gin-and-tonics or any other form of mind-numbing release.

This may all sound super-complicated. Is it complicated to believe you must invent your own motherroot?

Yet with or without all this intellectual mediation, the link grew between me and the little sheep, the brute deep animal fact of connection, its contours surprising and self-created.

Let us say you felt most at home mothering your daughters in places where foreignness made more sense. The fun of mothering daughters outside home! Unite as perpetual travelers, jostle, explore with a delight no dictionary can contain.

Let us also say that apart from motherhood, you might belong to that chorus born with a sense you don't belong. And thus, even apart from ecological virtue, it makes sense to wear the clothes of others: you are finding yourself in something that doesn't belong to you.

The estimable Gordon Lish, writing teacher, father of one, replicating the suffering of his youth in which he was mercilessly teased for psoriasis, famously made his students read stories aloud, stopping them and even kicking them out of his lauded workshop when he believed they came to a false word. He sent someone out—crying?—when she used the word *parenting*. This is how you feel, writing about *parenthood*. You could be ejected. Your clothes are borrowed. You don't even know the right language.

Come back, if you will, to that conversation with the daughter about the dusty used-clothes store. Our conversation continued:

No, daughter said, *this used-clothes store had a completely different atmosphere. And there was that boy, the crazy one with matted hair, linked with the refugees.*

That guy who helped us go undercover to help at the refugee camp? But he was so together!

Not that one!—teenage scorn has a polite correlate, an emphasis on nuance, which shouts at deaf parent: *Can't you see? Those two exist on different sides of a spectrum!*

And then the memory returns, jeweled as her shirt: the boy with his beauty smudged by street hardship who had started in, as so many have done, confidingly:

and you know that a person can start to speak and touch on his loved ones and his former loved self. And you watched him assume the contours of another face, because time folds, memory yearns backward, the spiral of life pretty much assures that one period of time will have very specific correlates with more than one prior period.

And yet because memory will always play trickster, whether or not this is what the boy said, what I recall is this story: early in a poor family, his looks made nearby aunties say he would easily have a Bollywood career. At birthdays, he would be prodded to dance, to act, he could do it all! On the strength of everyone's conviction, he palmed a one-way ticket to Bollywood where he found in Mumbai nothing but tricksters and hucksters and ended up living in slums outside the grand hotels. All the while, he was troubled by the way legacy seemed to have backfired. An employment agency sent him to Greece where he was mistreated by a wealthy family, and his papers stolen. He ended up, as people can, in Cyprus. Not an official European Union refugee, he had just landed on an isle where people stared at him.

His hope like anyone's, like yours or mine, was that any place would see his inner worth and recognize him. *Can you help me with a job?*

Let's go talk to the refugee people. Thinking of the hepcat pierced workers with gentle faces in their tiny bare air-conditioned office. Along crumbled ochre stone corridors that stand as testament to every kind of failed institution, we kept talking, and he stayed quite voluble: the aunties, obstacles to making it as a screen star, why his best chance lay around the corner.

We entered the AC freeze of an international outpost, a room dedicated to offering newcomers homes and jobs; he perked up, but when we said goodbye, he fell mute as if disconsolate, staring at the forms thrust his way by the hepcats, and looked—in his studied regard of papers asking which skills were his, what he might be qualified to do—as if that room made him so much smaller, more aware of belonging and its lack.

Weeks later, in a brisk supermarket, all matted hair and chalky jaw, he was seen again, weighing a bag of potatoes and a bag of apples, items of the new and old worlds, and when almost no one was looking, he thrust both the cookable and raw into his satchel. The hepcats, it turned out, had never quite helped, and it may have been that the cold sterility of bureaucracy, the fretwork required at the threshold of future belonging, rebuked the very strategy used to arrive at the brink.

The star could not arrive, the means rejected the ends rejected the means, the telos demanded a better present. Your shared dream had seen him before a vast audience, singing with such talent, crooning his heart toward the skies which had recognized him, plucked him from obscurity, granted him his wishes: at least that he could find some streetside audience.

Art (mode, manner, skill, weapon) almost could redeem all. That boy and the beauty that sent him out on a quest. *Remember that boy?* your daughter in her jeweled shirt asks. How could you not? Amnesia is a privilege which this survival screed forces you to abandon, despite your best intentions. Roland might have counseled the boy that he was right to fear structure, that stepping over another's preconceived threshold itself can be a theft, and that belonging is always invented, because what trust can you always have about being enfolded in another's body?

Image

There is something about gluttony that bothers you, daughter #1 says, after the birthday of daughter #3. Perhaps, instead, empty rite disturbs. As a child, ignored but for the moment celebrating your birth. In adolescence, you were offered dinner out! Imagine a lowlit restaurant and your mother's love of the ceremonial: inner dissociation found its locus. If the cosmos was a tent pulled tight, you floated somewhere, inside or out, it didn't matter. No gravity to your being. Eat all the tempura you want, nothing changes. You cannot consume love. Yet knowing the script called for a particular performance: happiness?

You want to be appreciated, says daughter #1.

Not because of daughters' table manners, you would rather offer them mangos sloppy with juice and eat in the shade by a trickling brook than get them stiff-backed in a restaurant too fancy.

I used to like luxury, says middle daughter. *Now I'm aware who or what this might displace. What all this might feed or do for someone.*

Once you had a friend, of the isle of Manhattoes, a warm connective person, who meant so well, equipped with wonderful ideals even as her status climbed, and she could not help it: her manner altered so radically, a rip in the universe, whenever she took you along for a fancy lunch or dinner. As she approached the front staff of any restaurant—reservation clerk, the take-out person, the maître d'—you shivered. To hear someone speak with such imperial assumption stripped all pleasure from consumption.

So often you wished to do it all, aiming to be unstinting, free-hearted: to offer them beautiful birthdays, their father somewhere near the punchbowl, creating fun for them until you collapsed. How often did the marriage feel as if you had burnt yourself to forest floor so he could waltz in like a happy bear, dancing over charred remains and enjoying low-hanging fruit? After the divorce, he chooses your secret special spots with the children as sites for himself to celebrate their birthdays, teaching them poker by a river. Avoid focusing on despoilage. You would do anything to love and outrun his message. The problem being that these two impulses war. You cannot love if your heart is scared. You cannot become the thing you wish to be—loving mother—if your fists are clenched and you can no longer recognize yourself. *Reactive abuse,* one friend diagnoses your case, *you have to get out ahead of reaction. Respond, yes. React, no.*

The image crumbles in
memory and moment both. The red wax
of the slice of birthday cake
melted on its plate without me.

Unknowable

Late night under a half-moon, no child in sight, you release the praying mantises you had ordered (natural way for ticks to be consumed) that had been hatching in a pair of plastic drinking glasses. Perhaps releasing them from their plastic home too soon, before they mate. Your newish beau had implored you let them out: *if they lack enough to eat, they will eat one another, become cannibals.* Alone, you let them out under the prune-plum tree you tried planting with your newish beau and ecotenant, the tree a European genus called hardy for this region, meant for human neighbors and your children to consume, but which already has been speckled with original neighbors, leaf maggots leaving a lacework behind. It is not clear who will survive all the transplantation of this time.

Next morning, no praying mantis in sight, one daughter comes like a snaggle-toothed renegade from her father's house to plant tomatoes doomed for the dumpheap she had found in her garden nursery job. Her handiwork: around the hill on which the parsonage sits, staked like wayward souls, planted well and poorly now are legions of poor starters, dark-horse tomato plants to whom she has performed outreach, stuck into the clay earth around the parsonage. Who dares grow from such difficult soil?

From your office of the summer morning kitchen, pondering the various unknowables of right now—why was x excluded from y gathering, what will happen in the world of health or politics or street or even this house—the legacy of your mother appears. Her belongings slammed up in the driveway, arrived in a dented pod. Let it be said that the homeland's cheery, sleepy movers, members of a moving collective who received the government's float funds, did their best but did not tie down your mother's legacy, now strewn and broken all around inside the pod, as true a metaphor for what the dead leave the living as any.

A wealthy person tells you a story about belongings coming to own the heirs: someone he knows ended up slave to the obligations required by an historic family house. *And the siblings also ended up practically married to the house so that no one married successfully,* he says, whatever success means, yet in this case: no mating, no later families, no future tenders for a dwelling that ended up outside the family.

In your house, recycling plastic from the vanished mantises' home, you don't want to become slave to your belongings.

But now in the living room you are a slave to the belongings of your family's past: a pillar stands from your mother's old life. (Don't look back if you don't wish to become a pillar of salt.) Open up bubble wrap to find the kitschy painting of villagers you had misread within her context. Back in that workaholic paradise, you had seen them as happy; now, opening the picture, you see them as bone-tired. The distinct glamor of her perfume fills the house.

The eldest daughter, tomato-strewer, cries at the arrival of the dented pod. It had escaped her visceral ken: grandparents' home? Her tears induce some last-ditch insanity: what if you had bought out Uncle Rick and your brother so as to give kids the illusion of a pillar that never bends? The myth of permanence. You cannot do it. Ridiculous, impossible, and yet the flare crosses, when all the wise minds of your contemporary moment and greater moment, whether poor or not, say to let grasping go.

Your mother loved pillars, stairs, hierarchies: bearing her cane, leaning on banisters, learning to walk so soon after the first stroke. Eternal, sweet-faced student, determined to improve. Careful, up each stair at the nursing home. Holding on to aspiration itself. Is it not remarkable and also ultimately unknowable the way each of us finds a way to stare down our own personal Armageddon?

The praying mantises, hung suspended as potential in their little egg, are nowhere to be seen. Perhaps they will have their meander and in some ten years their spawn will return to improve our neighborhood, and where will we all be then? We have created our plans and what will remain is the twist of our past with any word used to conjure it.

Outcomes

This is a time in which our
pretense at discreteness is
revealed: forget *je suis un autre*
there is no other,
we cannot help but stay
among ourselves.

Jealousy

He has not seen anyone for five months who is not related to me, and she comes by, the former childhood star, and he has told me two things: that friends of his are coming by, and they will aim to take the puppy for a walk. When she comes, contrary to his usual genial welcoming of me into his sphere, he doesn't tell me to come to the door. He is cute with hair tied, the smile from his maternal line beaming at them.

One daughter in the parsonage spies on his backwoods visitor and sees her squat to use the facilities of forest floor.

Next day, I take puppy with daughter #1 to the puppy obedience class. Daughter has been in a relationship with someone who chides her for her way of treating the puppy; who talks to her about being the alpha, who holds the dog's head to the ground, commenting on her treatment of new puppy. At the class, we are given clickers. In class, we are to decide on a task for the human who is led out of the door: touch the purse, bow before the hoop, whatever it is. The humans are confused; the point of this is to show that, using learning theory, one must reward good behavior. To give the treat to the dog before she barks, that we are alert to the door opening. The trick is that one must be sensitive to what can perturb our animal: what does she perceive as a threat?

Does the dog trainer love animals or how she controls them? And yet she is gentle with daughter. Perhaps to do this job well, one must suffer fools gladly. So seems to be the case for what is being asked of all of us in this moment. We misperceive signals, weak or strong, we must give one another grace notes of acceptance. And that we reward wrong behaviors with negative attention: what can one do with that? *You are everything to me,* says new beau, *you are my mate for life.* While you imagine the movie star's forest floor, her latest screen. Let your mind frolic where it will but also give up its crueler habits, here in a time when the outside has shrunk to the scale of the doors of your heart.

I-love-you

He sits by me in the outdoor
watercolor class I teach for
the neighbors and is a beautiful
presence. Who needs pigment
diluted by water?

The next morning, the heat
is intense and yet I reach for
him. Intensify, intensify.

Languor

You lie in the field of
exquisite, a river valley
to which you have driven,
a fleecy Saturday

of our float and you
know heat: some instant flash
peeling away memories, offering
so many states,

all those
years of that and this
pealing in the cathedral of
trees. If you pay attention to the

minute teaching of heat, there is
pleasure to be had: a rocket ship
through your past, down the center of
the earth, up above the trees, you

are left, luminous, unbounded, unaware when
the next bolt will pin you down.

Magic

The onscreen you was talking with an onscreen someone his age whom you wanted to bring into another partially screened conversation, this literacy project you started with the idea that it is good to share the powers of storytelling. (Let all gather around the campfire to gaze at stars and know awe.) Downstairs in the life called real, you wash up the fetid squalor of the welcome squash you cooked on his return, your beau having been gone a week, the chance for girlchildren to be solo with mother. Some guilt to the request for absence, some reparations within the yellowing squash, some metaphor to the yellow-wallpaper squalor: do you have the right to call a temporary cave around just you and cubs?

The guilt probably provokes the shadow-thought about someone else. (In class the day before, discussing a writer, you mentioned this concept: *The most dangerous person is the one who does not own his own shadow.*)

What, just because she's my age? You're my mate, he says, a breaking of the fourth wall, addressing the unspoken, and then goes into full recitative:

It's you I like,
It's not the things you wear,
It's not the way you do your hair
But it's you I like
The way you are right now,
The way down deep inside you
Not the things that hide you,
Not your toys
They're just beside you.
But it's you I like
Every part of you.
Your skin, your eyes, your feelings
Whether old or new.
I hope that you'll remember
Even when you're feeling blue

That it's you I like,
It's you yourself
It's you.
It's you I like.

Why do we find the childish so oddly fulfilling? (Because it speaks to the little wormwood of immaturity that tinges our personal absinthe.) Younger, you squinted uncertain at the sketchy screen: the performer Mister Rogers sang the song, faking it your way. An actor like all adults, he only pretended to see you while your seeing of him was the only possibility. He doesn't know me, you thought, as if angry at the artificial intelligence of it all. You believed no one could see into you, doomed to lurk outside, as if Frankenstein's own monster peeking into the routines of others.

Today the computer tech at the collapsing institute confides he hoped to find a girlfriend, yet, having been here some years, erasing one year because of the glittervirus, he feels less hope. A psychic told him to go to cities where emotional life lives more suppressed: say, Amsterdam or Montreal. That he wasn't in the right place. *You know me a little,* he says, *I am not always easy.*

But what is easy? The magic of the person who can recognize the vastness of nature and yet hold a hand with such warmth? The magic in your mate's hand after the Mister Rogers song; that you can guess the tiniest part of another which needs the greatest soothing. By some carnival trick, he offers it. That both of you feel seen by the greater eye of love at the same time. Is that not magic?

Yet in order not to be torn

By bulletholes, money, art, love, family, job, householding, say you leave briefly then with new love, to go to this artist island off the coast of Maine. Threaded into the story is the substrate of thermal energies beneath our feet which erupt. So much life lived in the premise of fiction: what if? If only?

You can spend life rehearsing dread, never full
in engaging, forever dancing with if-only-I-finish-
the-next-thing, imagining freedom
at the unreachable end, as in so many religions that magnetize
followers toward the cliff
-hanger of the end.

You could run amok off the cliff toward an illusion of freedom.

Say that just before you leave for the island, the pills given you by your drag-mother-friend-pharmacist suppress your body's defenses and cause your mood to be tenuous as an egg balanced on a tiny silver heirloom plate as you improvise modern dance backwards across a tightrope made of your past.

Say that on the island, you overfunction around dysfunction, the John Henry gift learned over years, the overweening mistake of hubris. You find a thornring tightening your head which no caffeine loosens.

Say that you feel you are trying to write this Roland book against imminent death: it must be writ, even if you tell it slant. Imagine that the bite sends you spiraling back through time to when humans were on the level of a bug and unable to make too many decisions beyond the binary: survival or death.

Say you gave a ride to a bad tick and, half-full on blood, it offered the lesson you were finally meant to get. Bacteria ate the neural pathways.

Ah it is not the tick, it is the bacteria, says the doctor, yet the medium also happened to be the message, Roland would have whispered into the ears of young McLaren. And the bacteria carried by Midas will burn out all the major and minor causeways of your brain.

So you, your face, your brain will freeze. Imagine the poor unknowing tick, Midas, just carrying its bacteria, wishing to eat like any of us, finding you hospitable, its bite injecting poison.

Imagine: after the first of long days in the emergency room, brain scanned inside a long chute colored as if from a 1970s scifi movie, you will feel grateful to all these long-hunched scientists who have created vessels for knowledge. And your new love shows mettle, canceling a trip out west. And the diagnosis arrives.

I am tanked,
ending as it were with half
a face lifted in a smile, unable
to move, an eye unable to close. The tragicomic
face of drama, a clown
immobilized.

As in a fable. No longer able to participate in the demands of others; I will have to shut down.

All this forward movement of life—the sundering, all—the overweening imagining of a new life and then no more forward, felled by a bug no bigger than this letter T.

In short, reader, a habit trained by generations of pogroms, the gesticulating monkey wishing to serve, the evolutionary habit of tend and befriend, now gone: I could not serve.

Know catastrophe and you must abandon all ideas of the self: not all-powerful, not abandoned, not independent, not defined by what it can push away.

I may have just buried my mother after her long intermittent sojourn through so many hospitals, her graciousness of a young girl and the affect she assumed: her dignity imperious, the calm suppliant arm presented to yet another nurse wishing to prod, poke, extract, wrap.

How her skin became a tender battleground, riddled and soft, still containing her after so many assaults. Knowing catastrophe, I catapulted into a period where, arm out, I understood mother's grace as an older person in the land of hospital.

Offer your body as if ready to be filled with buckshot. To become a veteran in a tunnel of ricocheting bullets in one of the acronym-laden tests we sling about: MRI or CT, spinal tap. To depend on the blandishments of strangers: meter readings, triage, the poisoned air of emergency rooms. Friends and family release you.

Back home in the parsonage, hole in arm, dangerous tube open and straight to my heart for a month, no bathing or swimming or exercise allowed, who arrived? Newish love came to enter and heal that vein:

Make yourself comfortable, he said each noontime
putting on music and offering pillows
wiping down plasticine mat for the saline/antibiotic/saline/heparin injections,
the (s)ash experience
pulling out four syringes
ripping open wipes
placing the tiny green plasticine hood
that would keep me from infection and death
Please find whatever works for you. Rest.

We were still somewhat new to each other, remember.

Rubbing alcohol wipes over the open nub in my arm toward the hole
that went straight to my heart and its whoosh
Tilting syringe upright

Careful in pushing so a tiny wet bubble appeared at the tip,
expunging its air before with great love he held my gaze and plunged
the four syringes direct into my vein
A Parisian morphine den would have had greater glamour
than our shooting gallery: but here he shot me up with the potential for life.

Are you able to trust anyone so totally?
Even if that person offers the softest kiss at the center of your forehead?
Were you ever that child who swore somewhere inside never to trust?
To never let the outside in?

Our metaphors about death and infection often revert to war.

Here, gentle soul, moth-trapper, disabler of mousetraps
with sweet focus he aimed to kill the intruder
who made me unable to find my mind's usual canals
even as I continued writing this thing meant
to keep us all going,
survival in our parsonage, aloft in days watery
and unmarkable. And yet (good news!) never
did I feel myself a burden.

Had I ever known this?

Reader's query, special for you, insert your own ideogram:
did I seize the chance to make of the crisis
opportunity, to remake
the mind, find myself anew, to know the joy of this
moment and the next?
To repattern the brain?
Or do we ever know when
performance inside our greatest
lesson begins or ends?

Pigeonholed

Let us say you once lived in a tight space and yet also overextended. Imagine you had to flee. How do you rework any neural pathway?

~~*Just touch my periphery*, you may have said, when it was your turn.~~
You may have been about to strike yourself through.
Or begged to hear a certain kind of song. Sing anything, songs of praise, you may have asked others.

~~*Let anyone say*~~
Did you ever have a clue how to soften your head?
Did you ever have a feeling all would collapse?

Let us say that once you started taking the med dispensed by the milk-skinned pharmacist, you start to herx, which, in a beautiful paradox, is a phenomenon named after his great-great-grandfather who discovered that, as illness starts to leave the body, as the bacteria start to die off, the patient might undergo worse symptoms for a while. Herxheimer foresaw our current state. Bring yourself to love and the illness starts to leave the body, which means that for a while you get worse, and yet this tunneling remains part of it, that we get worse for a while means there remains some greater hope of light.

You might not be able to keep the holiness of the I-Thou relation constant with anyone. You might not be able to keep that inexhaustible warm communion with the cosmos at the center of anything. There might be moments when you find yourself lost in seeing the thingness of life and everyone. The bills and chaos. But the waves of some particular love energy stay, rolling in and receding, beautiful tides, and because you let yourself trust, you might as well recognize: as if for the first time your heart becomes that home in which you wish to stay a while.

Ravishment

How can it be that in the great dusty sweep of time that there sprout fresh
moments: at the harvest festival, you rise
with your beau and three kids
to shake the lulav and etrog
in different directions, and there is
a timelessness your beau knows
in the eight minutes he has before he
has to leave, and you feel so
blessed with community, meeting
outdoors in the fall air, blessing
everything. You oil the pan later for dinner,
onion chopped, sprig of mint,
your mind perhaps not fresh but
at least ready.

Disreality

So many moments at the point of death are disreality.

To list them here: once you were on a plane and one of the wings, over which you were sitting, caught on fire. Goodbye to each person you loved, one second of that, and then the flight attendants started to run.

Once you had dengue fever, from a mosquito, and your consciousness lifted out of your body.

One time you saved a friend who had a tropical fever from nurses who kept saying the doctor was coming in an endlessly deferrable now.

One time a friend was killed and at that exact moment, elsewhere, in Jerusalem, you had to leave a class, laughing (and from this sprang all your future writing).

One hour your father was about to die, and your little two-year-old daughter knew it, she was quite insistent about people going into hospitals and never leaving.

One time before that, you woke as if with bricks on your chest the exact minute, a continent away, he had his heart attack.

One time you had a dream of your arms too long for your body and woke to hear your friend's baby had been born a little person.

One time you told fortunes on the sidewalk, as a twelve-year-old fictive huckster outside a Berkeley sidewalk café who could see people's deaths.

One time your daughter said she knew when people would die.

One time she saw your dead father walking around without his legs.

One time after her death your mother told you not to worry about minutiae, that the disreality of life near death is such thin tissue.

One time someone died and the spell over your writing lifted.

One time you chose to let in allies.

One time a bug bit you and your brain stopped.

One time someone tried to heal you and you aimed for trust.

One time you woke to a beautiful person wanting to cuddle in bed.

Just tell me you don't touch him when we're here. Just save it for the times when we're not here. This your daughter said in the life that has become yours.

The raised gardenbeds have arrived. A praying mantis and ladybug wait on the unopened box. You are trying to create structure from which life might spring. *A glance could suffice—ours—for the world to be eternally complete.*

~

Acknowledgments

To Carol Frederick, one of the world's greatest champions of art and heart, and her long-standing presence at the earthly paradise Art OMI, along with all the other directors.

To all those connected to Eastern Island Frontier/Norton Island residency including Mike Reilly, Lizzy, Steve, and Rosy Faver Dunn, and to the magic of the place in which this book found its form.

To Hambidge.

To David Rothenberg, who first risked for this, editor Evan Eisenberg, who entered with enthusiasm and insight, and to the memory of Howard Eisenberg.

To Randall Knoper, Jenny Adams, Joe Black, Jeff Parker, Sabina Murray, Lynne Latham, Tom Racine, Patty O'Neill, and Adam Zucker, as well as other colleagues in the MFA and the University of Massachusetts for research support.

To the lighthouse beam of agent Soumeya Bendimerad-Roberts along with Hannah Popal and Rhea Lyons.

To the enduring, bright tether of Amalena, Jeff Gyvingmore, and Larry Bensky, West Coast legendary activists.

To Sue and Mike Austin and Carol and Michael O'Day for their combined and individual Brookside warm intelligence. To Brenda Kahn, a mermaid and writer, Judith Silverstein, Mike Healy, a secret mayor, and all the Brookside writers.

To Sara Acker and Susannah Ludwig for illuminated hearts.

To Yael, Ana, and the yedidot.

To all the warm inspiration of those I do not mention here. To friends, neighbors, students, and all teachers.

To Andrea Scrima at *Statorec* who first culled and published this material, and later used it in the anthology *Writing the Virus* (Outpost 19), and helped it find perch in the New York Public Library audio vault as well as HERE Gallery (Manhattan) for a stop-motion collaboration with Luna Knightley.

To the fierce real help of Claire Bargout, Theo and Holly Black, Sylvia Brownrigg, Jim Carpenter, Carolyn Cooke, Dafney Dabach, Mariah

DeLeon, Margot Douaihy, Sharon Guskin, Debra Immergut, Maria Johnson, Emmy Kinarty, Rae Kootman and family, Amii LeGendre, Rami Margron, Laura Marshall, Josh Meidav and family, Elizabeth Rosner, Kevin Salem, Tara Shafer, Mila Sherman and family, Sheila, Kenny, and all Sonnenscheins, Pam Thompson.

To Michael Ravitch.

To all members of the medical profession who kept me alive, especially Gena Wilson, Jenn Goldstock, and Dr. Paz.

To Tyran Grillo, Colette McCormick, and designer Martin Pedanik, kind, patient, inspired.

To the enduring love of Lerners, Naparsts, Kinartys, Meidavs.

To the innomenence of Ben Richter and family.

To the beloved brilliant ever-unfolding gift of D and E.

Bibliography, background, citations

Barthes: A Lover's Discourse: Fragments, Roland Barthes, translated from the French by Richard Howard. Foreword by Wayne Koestenbaum. Hill & Wang, a division of Farrar, Straus and Giroux, New York. 1978.

Mourning Diary: October 26, 1977-September 15, 1979, Roland Barthes. Text established and annotated by Nathalie Léger. Translated from the French by Richard Howard. Hill & Wang, a division of Farrar, Straus and Giroux, New York. 2010.

Roland Barthes: A Biography, Louis-Jean Calvet, translated by Sarah Wykes, Indiana University Press, Bloomington and Indianapolis, 1995.

Barthes: A Biography, Tiphaine Samoyault, translated by Andrew Brown, Polity Press, Institut Francais, 2015.

Also of interest

All of Roland Barthes' work.

Barthes: A Very Short Introduction, Jonathan Culler, Oxford University Press, 1983.

Interdisciplinary Barthes, edited by Diana Knight, published for The British Academy by Oxford University Press. London, 2020.

Roland Barthes, by Patrick Mauriès, Aux Editions du Seuil, L'Imprimerie Floch, Mayenne, 1992.

Bringing Out Roland Barthes, by D.A. Miller, University of California Press, Berkeley, Los Angeles, Oxford, 1992.

A Barthes Reader, edited with an introduction by Susan Sontag, Barnes and Noble Rediscovers, by arrangement with Farrar, Straus & Giroux, 1982.

The Professor of Desire, by Steven Ungar, University of Nebraska Press, Lincoln and London, 1983.

List of illustrations

All images by Cecile Bouchier, except for a few by the author.